SHUNIAH-OGAMA

Money Boss

ROBERT SANDERSON TRUDEAU

 FriesenPress

One Printers Way
Altona, MB R0G 0B0
Canada

www.friesenpress.com

Although the novel draws on many historical events in the Nakina
District of Northwestern Ontario between the fall of 1972 and the
spring of 1977, the characters depicted are entirely the author's
construction.

ISBN
978-1-03-915566-4 (Hardcover)
978-1-03-915565-7 (Paperback)
978-1-03-915567-1 (eBook)

1. FICTION, THRILLERS, HISTORICAL

Distributed to the trade by The Ingram Book Company

To the Anishinaabe of the Blue Forest.

Table of Contents

Part Three

Part Four

The Ojibwa in Northwestern Ontario employed a term that defined their relationship with the Canadian government. They called the government officials the 'Shuniah-Ogama' or 'money boss'.

– Ojibwa elder

Part One

Chapter 1

THE COMMERCE OFFICER

(1)

It was a warm spring day in May 1976 in Grayson, north-western Ontario, Canada: a quiet day with hardly a soul in sight. On Main Street there was little traffic, except for a half-ton truck that drove past a number of older buildings, two hotels, and seedy rooming houses. Grayson, a former gold-mining town, had the look and feel of a Hollywood movie set. All that was missing was the director yelling "Action!" and the camera operator following the actors around as they each took turns speaking their parts.

Quietly sipping a cup of tea on the front porch of one of the rooming houses sat the new commerce officer for the Nakina District Department of Indian Affairs and Northern Development – 'the agency.' He was a pale, thin man worn out from having completed an introductory circuit of the nine district Indian communities.

Over four weeks, he had travelled in small float-planes to five villages far to the north, above the CN rail line, some halfway to Hudson Bay. Then, over two weeks, he had driven an Indian Affairs station wagon to

5

four off-highway settlements, one settlement alone two hundred and twenty kilometers to the east off Highway 11, and three others closer to Grayson.

In all nine communities he met with the chiefs and councils and took his time to explain who he was and what his role and responsibilities were in an organization he knew very little about. "My name is Rager," he said quietly to each group, "John Rager. I'm your new district commerce officer. As I understand it, my role is to encourage and support economic development in your community. I take that to mean I work in helping people to start their own businesses and the Council to obtain funding to undertake make-work projects."

He told them about himself. "Before joining Indian Affairs, I worked for three years with the Ontario Cooperative Development Association out of Sioux Lookout. I was a business advisor to different Indian-owned general stores. I know the struggles of starting and operating a business in a remote Indian community. I'm also an accountant with a CGA." He didn't mention all the companies he had worked for and the jobs he left, but he did tell them what he lacked. "I still have a lot to learn about Indian Affairs, the programs they offer, and how they operate. I hope I can be useful in helping you and your people achieve economic growth. I hope you get the results you want."

And then, unexpectedly, he listened to the chiefs and councils complain that his predecessor had done nothing but drink, chase women, and take bribes from the air charter company that serviced the Indian Affairs-owned

tourist camps – a make-work project for the five fly-in villages that did very little to create employment. They told
him that he should start by helping the villages to establish
their own development corporation to take over ownership of the tourist camps. One of the chiefs said pointedly,
"We can do much better, thank you." The chiefs and councils in the off-highway villages said they hoped he would
help them to secure long-term contracts from the forestry
companies which were doing very little but clear-cutting.

"Everyone makes money, but not us," is how one of
the younger chiefs put it. The Chief also said, "All those
Indian Affairs loan and contribution programs ask for
equity. We are a poor people; we don't have money – or
equity, as they put it – to access those programs. How can
our people start a business?"

As he reflected on his circuit of meetings on this bright
spring day, Rager thought, "I have a lot to learn, but I'll
figure it out as I go along."

Out of nowhere, a tall man approached. "What are you
doing on the porch, John?"

"Nothing, Frank – just thinking."

Frank nodded. "I was out all night and woke up in
the cemetery. I'd passed out lying beside a tombstone. I
thought I was dead. How I got there, I have no idea." The
man was a worker in a nearby lumberyard. He shook his
head, walked into the rooming house, and disappeared
into one of the rooms.

Rager finished his tea and went to his room, ate
breakfast in the shared kitchen, and decided to walk to
the office. He knew it was always best to do paperwork

on the weekends when no one else was around to disturb his thinking.

The Nakina Agency District Office was housed on the second floor of a red-brick federal building with a tattered Canadian flag out front, barred windows, and a post office on the first floor. The catholic church with its tall steeple loomed in the background behind the building. Rager walked up the stairs to the second floor. When he reached his small, cramped back office, where the smell of disinfectant permeated every inch of space, he opened the window to let in fresh air, sat down, and began to work his way through a stack of files.

He worked through the morning, broke for lunch, and returned to work on a business plan for an Indian man in one of the off-highway settlements. The man planned to start a trucking business but had very little in equity to invest. The Toronto regional official responsible for the Indian Small Business Loan Program had told him not to expect loan approval, but to apply anyways. "They seem to play a guessing game," Rager thought.

When it started to get dark, he returned to the rooming house, ate supper, and went to bed.

As he lay in bed, Rager began to dream of Helen. Three years earlier, his wife had left him, taking their son Sam with her to Edmonton and leaving only a note on the kitchen table – "Don't bother following." She was remarried now and had little to do with him. It was understandable – he was a difficult man, often moody, someone who drank more than he should, and he was good at hiding his feelings, perhaps too good.

He thought of the day when it all came to a boil – a silly day when he had shown how little he really cared for her until it was too late, until even regrets meant little.

(2)

In memory, Rager sees the lake, the sandy shore, the island with the long cedar trees reaching out over the water like giant ribs, and the sand bar where the loons and ducks swim. He had swum to the island and stayed a long time before leaving while Helen and Sam waited for him on an isolated public beach. At one time she had been pretty, but now Helen was overly thin and nervous; she was stuck in a miserable marriage and it showed on her face. She was reading a popular novel that allowed her to drift away into another world. Sam, a quiet boy with blue eyes, who had just turned five, played in the sand.

When Rager stepped out of the water and walked up, Helen placed the book down and looked up. She was angry and it was evident. "How was your swim?" she asked.

"Good," he replied.

"You know, I was worried silly; you were gone such a long time. Do you know that it was over three hours? But then, I suppose you don't care what I think, do you?"

"I thought it was only two hours..." He hesitated. "I'm not really sure how long, Helen, but I told you I'd be gone quite a while. I like to be alone – I need time to think. It helps me to clear my head."

"I don't know what it is about you, John, I really don't know. Who in God's name leaves his wife and son on an isolated beach in the middle of nowhere, with not a soul in sight, and goes off swimming, alone, out in the middle of a lake where he might drown, takes no life preserver, gone for over three hours, and doesn't bother to say a single word – except, 'I'm going swimming to the island, honey'? Who does that, John – who in God's name does that? Tell me one single person? No one – that's who! No decent living person, only you…only you...you son of a bitch! You're such a fucking bastard! Such a coward!" She began to cry softly.

"I know you don't care about me, you never have, and I doubt you care anything about Sam. You're so selfish, so very selfish. I don't have a clue who you are – I don't think anybody does. If you want to die, do it," she said. "If you want to be alone, just leave. But for God's sake, don't treat me like a fool." She was tired of his quiet silences, his long trips, his swimming off to be alone, and his binge-drinking. After six years of marriage, she knew nothing about the man would change – could not change. He was a stone statue when it came to sharing his feelings.

"I'm sorry you feel that way," Rager said.

"That's all you have to say?"

"I am sorry."

"I doubt that very much."

Helen continued to cry. It was the sort of crying Rager had witnessed with his mother when she had lost a book-keeping position in one of the needle trade companies in the east end of Montreal, where they lived over a convenience store, a widow and her small frail boy. He stared off in the distance, unable to think of how to reply. "I need a beer," he said.

"You always do."

Helen stopped crying, picked up the novel, and began reading as though nothing had happened.

Rager walked to the car with the broken door that was never fixed, the radio that never played properly, and the window that was always cracked – the things he would always promise to repair and never get around to repairing. Thinking Helen might want to drink, he took two bottles of beer from the case, opened them, and brought one over to where she sat.

"I brought you a beer," he said.

"I don't want to drink," she replied. "Not now, not ever, and certainly not with you."

"If that's how you feel, then don't."

"Go away – please, just go! I don't want to talk."

He drank one of the beers. Then he walked up to Sam, who was playing in the sand.

"What are you doing, Sam?"

"I'm building a lake, Daddy."

"Is that a house in the middle of the lake?"

"Oh, you're so silly. How could a house float in the middle of a lake? Don't you know this is your island – the one you swim to when we come here? Is it a nice island, Daddy?"

"Yes, it's a very nice island, Sam."

"Is it a big island?"

"No, it's very small; it hardly has any room to walk around. There's just enough room to lie down and stretch out, and when you do, your feet touch the water. But it's a beautiful island with warm sand, and there are always ducks and loons nearby."

"What do you do on the island?"

"I listen to the loons. They talk to me, they say, 'Hello, John, good to see you.' They're always very polite."

"Are there many loons?"

"Only a Mommy, a Daddy, and two baby loons."

"Can I go to the island?"

"Yes, Sam, when we get a motorboat."

"A big boat?"

"Yes, a big boat, something we can all sit in together." Rager continued talking, drawing out the lie by describing the boat.

The boy picked up a stone and pretended it was a motor boat. He moved it back and forth over the sand. "Can I drive the boat, Daddy?"

"Yes, Sam; our boat will have a steering wheel so you can drive, and there'll be seats in the front and back so we can all go as a family. But you can be the captain and drive the boat."

The boy pretended to steer the imaginary boat. "I'm going to drive fast," he said. He stood and began to run back and forth along the beach. As he did, he made the sound of a roaring outboard motor. "Rumm...rummm!"

"Don't crash!" Rager yelled.

"I won't!"

The boy ran up and down the beach until he was out of breath. When he sat down, he gasped, "I...I...was going fast...and the loons...the loons...were chasing me, all the time they were chasing me, but I got away...I got away." After he caught his breath, Sam asked, "Will you play with me, Daddy?"

It was a hot day with hardly any breeze. Using sand and pebbles, Rager helped the boy build an island with two loons on a lake. He told the boy that loons were lonely and not like other birds who lived in flocks, and beautiful, perhaps the most beautiful of all waterfowl, and their cry the most special cry of all – always piercing, haunting, and lonely. He told the boy the legend of how the loon was given a band of white on its neck by granting the gift of sight to a blind medicine man and receiving a necklace in return.

The boy listened and believed everything his father told him. When he finished telling the story, Sam asked, "Daddy, will we always be here?"

"Yes, Sam, as long as we want to."

"We won't move again?"

"No – never again." Rager turned to see if Helen could hear, but she was reading her book, unaware of what he had said. "I think we'll be here a long time," he said.

"I don't like it when we move."

"I know, son."

"I love you, Daddy."

"I love you too."

A week later, they were gone.

(3)

When Rager woke, it was the middle of the night. He thought, "I never expected that things would turn out this way, with me living alone in a rooming house and working for an agency that does very little but play tricks on Indians." But he knew that Helen had nothing to offer him, nor he to her, and he was a poor example to his son, the only one he loved. After three years with the Ontario Cooperative Development Association, thinking he might do more good working from within the government than a non-profit, he decided to join the agency. After his circuit of the nine district villages, he wondered if he had made a terrible mistake.

Rager climbed out of bed and walked over to the open window. When he looked out, he saw night hawks fluttering in trees, moonlight falling across rooftops, and a drunk Indian man waving his arms, stumbling out of an alley. A half-block away, the water tower stood over the houses and buildings like an inflated balloon; it was a miserable, grey thing with "Grayson" blazoned across like an advertisement for misery. When he went back to bed and tried to sleep, he slept poorly, thinking of what had been lost to him forever. Only when he remembered the beach and the small boy did he seem truly at peace.

Chapter 2
THE NUN'S LETTER

It was a late Monday morning. Dark, ominous clouds crowded the sky over Grayson, but the Indian Affairs District Manager paid no heed to the thought of a thunderstorm. The sixty-four-year-old gentleman with the white hair and the soft round tummy, who sprayed his hair every morning with Monsieur Conte, carried no umbrella or raincoat after hitting a few golf balls in the municipal golf course in the early hours. At that time of day, there were no other players on the course and he could do as he wished, placing the golf ball where it suited him and cheating on the score – not that it mattered. It was simply a game, he thought; a silly game played with a stick and a ball. Did he really have to keep a score card? He could shoot rabbits if he wished – not that he wanted to shoot rabbits, but there it was: he could shoot rabbits, or play with a stick and a ball. After playing an hour, Mr. Reed had taken his time to eat a proper breakfast and change his clothes. He wore a plain grey suit, white shirt, and tie.

Given his age and appearance, when he left his government-bungalow he might easily have been mistaken for an older high school teacher approaching retirement – if only he had attempted to be a different person. But then, Mr. Reed was always pleased with himself, could almost whistle, and the thought of being anyone else never entered his mind, not even once. He also felt that it was an obligation never to be noticed, to blend in.

The district manager walked along Main Street. When he came to the rail line, he crossed and took no notice of the shuttered CN train station. No train had stopped in Grayson since the last gold mine had closed. The station would soon be torn down, leaving an empty lot, and for what?

When Mr. Reed came to the small, red-brick federal building, he paid no notice to the sign outside that read "Post Office" with no mention of an Indian Affairs District Office on the second floor. It had been that way for five years, ever since the agency first opened the office and appointed Mr. Reed district manager. But it never bothered him that there was no proper sign. Did it really matter? Not really, he thought. He often said to those who worked in the office, those who came and went like the change in the seasons, "We are not the Ontario Provincial Police, with officers in uniforms running in and out of police cars and giving out tickets. No: we are the Department of Indian Affairs and Northern Development. We work quietly and, more importantly, discreetly. We have no need to advertise our presence. No, indeed, absolutely no need." And that was the end of any discussion about the lack of a sign.

Mr. Reed also said to any new officials, especially those who came with an attitude for change, "Never make a promise you can't keep. Preferably, say nothing. People don't need to know anything about what we do or don't do – the less the public knows, the better." In Mr. Reed's mind, if you never made a promise, no one could criticize you. You could simply say, "I never said I would do that," and that would be the end of it. You simply never gave them a target and kept moving. Except that Mr. Reed never did move on: he sought no promotion or transfer and stayed in the district office like a bad tenant who never pays rent. He was a permanent fixture as much as the worn-out, stained government-issued desks, the ashtrays full of cigarette butts, the smell of disinfectant in the early morning after the cleaners had done their work, and the grey, ugly faces of middle-aged men sitting around a table eating ham and cheese sandwiches at lunch.

As he approached the post office, late as usual, the white-haired man in the grey suit walked around to the back alley and up the fire escape to the back door. It was always best to avoid the front entrance where an Indian might be lurking waiting to make a complaint. The list of Indian complaints concerning the villages was exhausting: the need for more and better housing; more welfare; the lack of water and sewage service; the need for school expansion; Indian Affairs' obligation to pay for funeral expenses – a number of Indians pointed to Treaty rights and said the government should pay for burial – and so on. As he always did, Mr. Reed crept up the fire escape and entered through the back door like an aging government spy, tiptoed down the corridor to his front office, entered, shut the door quickly, and sighed with relief. "Why am I always burdened?" he thought. "Why am I always so frightened? Do I not have anything to really fear?" Or so he thought.

Mr. Reed began to read through the weekly onion skin copies – the "flimsies" – of district correspondence. It was his primary way of staying abreast of district activities without having to hold staff meetings; instead, he simply read what others were writing, gleaning just enough to know what they were doing or planning to do. It was slow, ponderous, and often challenging work – looking up the occasional word in a dictionary or a regulation in a policy and procedures manual that often left him more confused than enlightened. However, Mr. Reed never left anything to chance or misinterpretation. After all, the district budgets were limited and needed constant monitoring. He often said to the district officers, "We can't simply hand out funding to the Indian villages, no matter how great the need. It has to be done properly, within approved budgets, and according to proper channels and procedures. We can never assume we know best. We have to be respectful of our superiors; they have the responsibility and authority to make the important decisions, and we implement those decisions like good soldiers. We are also not a bank with an endless amount of money. We are one agency within a large federal government bureaucracy, no more than the front line in a long line of officials leading back to Ottawa." The capital city intimidated Mr. Reed as though he were a humble priest speaking about Rome.

As Mr. Reed read through the flimsies, he noticed that the newly built Fort Moore agency cabin had not been painted. He immediately phoned the district supervisor of construction and capital projects to give him direction. "Freddy," he said, "I want the cabin painted a plain colour – nothing extravagant. Do you understand?" He repeated himself. "Nothing extravagant. Can I make it any clearer?"

"Yes, Bob, the cabin will be painted a dull, unattractive brown, the window frames off- white, the door dark grey, absolutely nothing bright to draw attention." The supervisor had said this a number of times, but Mr. Reed – as he often did – forgot.

"Good!" he replied. Whatever else they talked about – the size of the cabin, the furniture and new appliances, or the ever-increasing cost of construction – was quickly dealt with and forgotten. If need be, Mr. Reed could forget almost anything.

As the days dwindled and summer came to an end, Mr. Reed increasingly thought of his pending retirement. In four months and ten days he would take his final walk out of the office and not bother to look back. Five years was a long time to be a district manager – too long, he thought. He often wondered what else he might have done. Then one day he realized, as though it were a bolt of lightning, "Why, there is nothing else I could have done. A district manager in a remote Indian Affairs district is simply perfect for my temperament. I should be thankful." And so, he was.

But then, as events unfolded, he read the copy of an unexpected letter that was addressed to David Stewart, the

Ontario Indian Affairs Regional Director General (RDG) and Mr. Reed's immediate supervisor, and Mr. Reed knew it was serious. At that very moment, he phoned the new district commerce officer and asked to meet him in the afternoon. "John, I need to see you," he said. "It is rather important. Let's make it two o'clock in my office."

(2)

At two o'clock, Rager knocked on Mr. Reed's door. "Come in," the district manager said. He walked in and took the chair in front of the older man's desk. The dark lines under his eyes and blotched skin did little to conceal Rager's recent drinking and lack of sleep. "I'm glad we're able to meet," said Mr. Reed. "I know you have a lot on your plate, what with being new to the district and having to meet all the chiefs and councils. I know how travel can wear a man down. Think of it like this: You've already completed your first circuit, and for the rest of the year you won't have to return more than once. In my experience, a letter is often all you have to send instead of having a meeting." He gave a weak, pathetic smile before coming to the issue at hand. "Well, let's get down to business. I have a serious matter on my plate; it's something I can't gloss over. I would have asked Gordon Hughes to handle the problem, but he's far too busy with his other duties. So, I thought of you, what with you being new and ready to take on new adventures."

Gordon Hughes was the district supervisor of local government and the official responsible for advising the chiefs and councils on matters pertaining to governance.

Mr. Reed had hired Gordon two years earlier because of his experience as a Hudson's Bay store manager in remote Indian villages. He was a crude Welshman, often yelling and swearing. "You should know that when I'm gone, Gordon will likely become the district manager," Mr. Reed said. "I can't think of anyone more suitable." Mr. Reed was due to retire in January.

Rager did not think much of the Welshman as a suitable replacement, but he offered no reply.

Mr. Reed produced a typed letter from a file. He held it up. Rager could see that it was long and carefully typed with a masthead bearing a crucifix. "This is a copy of a letter that was sent to David Stewart, the regional director general. It's from a Catholic nun named Sister Marie Brunelle, who spent six months last year in Windsor House providing family counselling. Her letter is quite disturbing. She accuses the department of every imaginable problem in the village – the violence, drinking, poverty, lack of housing, and so much more. I don't think there's anything she misses. More importantly, she accuses district officials of taking bribes. Of course, all of this is absolute and utter nonsense. She might just as well blame us for the bad weather. Anyway, you can read the letter and judge for yourself. He handed the letter over to Rager and he began to read:

> Dear Mr. Stewart:
> My name is Sister Marie Brunelle. I am a member of the Sisters of Charity of the Ottawa house. I am also a trained social worker who has worked in many different

countries throughout Africa, often the poorest, and most recently, after the last famine, Biafra. I write this so you know that I am no stranger to poverty, hopelessness, and government indifference to the suffering of its weakest citizens. I am also a proud Canadian and someone who believes in the sharing of our good fortune with those who have so little.

Last January, I was asked by my superior, Mother Theresa, to travel to Windsor House. As you know, Windsor House is a remote Ojibway Indian village in the vast Hudson Bay lowlands, a region of Canada with no roads or towns, no means of travel except either by plane or freighter canoe, and no resident police. The village is one of nine within the Nakina Indian Affairs district. At the time, I was asked to provide family counselling in the hope of reducing the drinking and violence that has plagued Windsor House for several years. The request came from the local priest, Father Benoît, an Oblate of Mary Immaculate who has served the region for nearly fifty years. Father Benoît is seventy-eight, a long-time resident of Windsor House, and a man with a heart condition who will soon have to leave the village permanently for medical treatment. A lay brother, Brother André, works with Father Benoît, but he too will leave the village.

In the six months I lived and worked in Windsor House I discovered the following:

The village has a long and troubled history. Up to the 1950s, there were only the Catholic mission and the Hudson Bay post while the Ojibwa who lived in surrounding outpost camps would only visit the village to trade furs, purchase supplies, or attend church. At the time and up to the present, they were forced to send their children to residential school. For many, this was a traumatic experience where many suffered often physical, emotional, and in some cases, sexual abuse. I believe it to be one of the underlying causes of depression, thoughts of suicide, violence, and drinking among the villagers today. I can only add that those who operated the residential schools have much to answer for – if not in this world, then the next. I would point out that although Father Benoît encouraged the parents to send their children to residential school, he later became one of the strongest proponents of building a school in the village. Unfortunately, the school offered only grades one to four, resulting in older children continuing to attend residential school. The village school has been closed for over a year.

In 1955, after the government built a small school and a nursing station, and began offering housing, the village grew rapidly. By 1972, there were 432 Ojibwa living in Windsor House, approximately half were Catholic and half Anglican. That year, however, a member of the Anglican community had a vision that the world would end on Easter Sunday. When the prediction failed, the Anglicans left Windsor House and established a new village forty-two kilometers north, named Big Beaver House. At that point, after considerable discussion, Indian Affairs agreed to provide the new village with all the programs and services they previously enjoyed. Those who remained in Windsor House, namely the Catholics, were not so fortunate. They were left with vacant houses, a half-empty school, and a cut in programs and services that was far in excess to what was justified by the decline in population alone. In short, the Catholics were punished for an event that was not of their making.

Currently, Windsor House is heavily dependent on government welfare as a primary source of income with almost ninety percent of families relying on welfare – while government attempts at creating a local economy have been, to say the least, a dismal failure. I will cite you but three examples:

In 1962, the mission established a small portable sawmill to produce lumber from local timber. They saw the sawmill as a means of providing lumber for housing construction and to create local employment. In the beginning, the sawmill was subsidized by Indian Affairs, but in 1970 the department decided the lumber was not up to their standards and they cancelled the subsidy. This resulted in the closure of the sawmill, a loss of local employment and income, and the import of lumber at much higher cost.

In 1965, the Department of Manpower began offering training programs including heavy equipment operator, house repair, bookkeeper, and adult education, which continued until 1973 when the programs were cancelled because of a lack of work for those trained – after all, how many heavy equipment operators or bookkeepers does a small village need, especially a village without roads or any businesses? The Department of Manpower apparently never gave thought to where people would find employment once they were trained.

Starting in the 1960s, Indian Affairs built a number of tourist camps to provide seasonal work as fishing guides, cooks, and camp attendants for the five fly-in district villages, including Windsor House. The camps, however, were poorly administered by district officials to the point that the air charter airline transporting the sports fishermen to the camps earned far more in revenues and profits than the villagers who worked in the camps. According to the villagers, district officials take bribes from the airline (the Mensen Air Charter Company) for the contracts, while other district officials take bribes for construction, fuel supply, and even the transport of children to the residential schools.

The living conditions in Windsor House are, to say the least, deplorable. Houses are poorly constructed, and today many suffer with mold. As I already mentioned, the primary school has been closed for over a year. Why? Because no teachers are willing to work in a school with a broken sewer line, broken doors and windows, and a furnace that leaks oil and deadly fumes. The village has no sewage system: villagers are forced to rely on privies. This is a serious problem in the spring when run-off from the privies travels into the lake, the primary source of village drinking water, which leads to diarrhea and sickness. The village has no piped water, let alone a water treatment plant. Villagers must walk to the lake to bring back water in pails. In the winter, when the lake freezes over, they use an auger to cut a hole in the ice for water, often filling a forty-five-gallon drum which they tow by snowmobile.

Because of the lack of water, laundry and bathing are often neglected, which leads to babies and small children suffering with scabies, often causing permanent disfigurement. Only government buildings are connected to water and septic fields – buildings that are often vacant because district officials seldom visit Windsor House and, as I have already mentioned, the school has been closed for over a year.

The villagers use wood stoves to heat their homes. No one has or can afford oil heat – except, of course, the government. All government buildings – school, teacher's residences, agency cabin, and nursing station – and the Hudson's Bay store and manager's residence, essentially all the white establishments, are heated by oil furnaces with fuel either brought in by tractor train or, at much greater expense, by plane.

Drinking and public drunkenness often reach epidemic proportions. The pattern is always the same. Someone arranges for a friend to purchase liquor (usually cases of cheap whiskey at the government-run liquor outlet in Grayson) and charter a plane (usually a DE Havilland Beaver or Cessna 185 because of the lower cost). When the liquor arrives, the drinking begins throughout the village. You will see a man or woman drinking a bottle of whiskey as though it were pop and then stagger around until he or she passes out unconscious. There is no such thing as a moderate drinker. Men and women drink until there is nothing left or they pass out. When there is no whiskey, the villagers make home brew, while children resort to gas-sniffing.

In the six months I spent in Windsor House I recorded the following violent incidents. I would point out that that after the Anglicans left in 1972, the population in Windsor House declined to 206 people, of which 202 are Ojibwa. Out of this small population:

- Three men raped a ten-year old girl. I spoke with the girl before she was medevacked to the Sioux lookout Regional Hospital for treatment.
- A drunk man chased his wife with an axe through the village, caught her, and beat her unconscious. When she recovered, he took her to an outpost camp. She was never heard from or seen again.
- A teenage boy burned down a house because he had nothing better to do. He told the Ontario Provincial Police officer who interrogated him, 'I like to see things burn.'
- During a recent Sunday mass, a drunk man appeared with a shotgun and threatened to shoot Father Benoît. This was only prevented when a parishioner disarmed the man.

In all these incidents the OPP never laid charges because no one was willing to testify for fear of reprisal or the mistaken belief that the culprit might change for the better. Currently there are five villagers serving jail terms in the south, either in provincial or federal jails, and the number would be much higher if charges had been laid in the incidents I described above. I must point out that Windsor House has no resident police officer because the provincial government classifies the village as an 'unrecognized community' – which means the OPP only arrive after a violent incident. Windsor House has no holding cell, so when the police do arrive and make an arrest, they either tie the prisoner to a tree or lock the prisoner in a shed with no ventilation or toilet except a tin can. In so many words, prisoners are treated no better than farm animals.

Currently, Windsor House has no effective leadership. The chief and council often stay in their outpost camps or, when the drinking begins, they hide in the bush in outright fear. They also have minimal decision-making power, while district Indian Affairs officials retain all the power – for example, the officials alone make all decisions pertaining to funding and spending and, for that matter, closing the school.

I have written your district manager, Mr. Reed, on more than one occasion asking for help. All I ever received was a brief letter informing me that district budgets are limited, and policing is a provincial responsibility. In so many words, your manager tells me that he will do nothing. I must point out that Mr. Reed seldom, if ever, visits Windsor House and when he does, he does not even bother to meet with the chief and council. Father Benoît told me that Mr. Reed once travelled to Windsor House, walked around, and took photos as though he was a tourist. Another time, he arrived on a charter with a group of officials, only consulting with the school janitor and band administrator before leaving. I leave it to you to ask why.

You might easily wonder why anyone stays in Windsor House. In reality, they have no choice. Those who leave do so in the mistaken belief they will find work and better living conditions in the south. Instead, they face discrimination and a lack of affordable housing, and with few financial resources, education, or skills, they soon return.

Mr. Stewart, I trust you hear my voice. I speak for a small Ojibwa village in the northern hinterland of Ontario, a village where people are condemned to suffer and die needlessly. I ask you to remember that they are your brothers and sisters, and I ask you to act in good conscience.

I remain your humble servant. In the name of our Lord and Savior, Jesus Christ,

Sister Marie Brunelle, SCO.

Rager looked over at Mr. Reed. The district manager attempted to hide his feelings.. At first his eyes appeared like those of a child seeking forgiveness. But then they became cold and distant, as though any thought of sympathy for the village was replaced with a feeling of fear and disgust. "Of course, she's exaggerating," he said. "I've been to Windsor House many times. I should know, shouldn't I?" Mr. Reed failed to mention that on one of those trips he had hidden in the agency cabin and pretended there was no one to meet in the village. Meanwhile, the supervisor of local government who was travelling with him met Father Benoît and the federal nurse to gather what information he could on projects and to write a report.

In reality, Mr. Reed knew very little about the village, its long-troubled history, or its actual needs, except for what he read in the flimsies. But over the years, the district officials continued to avoid the village, so there was less to read about. In many ways, as far as Mr. Reed was concerned, Windsor House didn't exist.

Mr. Reed's voice began to rise. "And these accusations of district officials taking bribes? Well, let me tell you that they're all lies, gross lies, easy to say but hard to prove." Then he added what had to be said: "Nevertheless, her accusations could hurt the district office and ruin my reputation."

He hesitated. When he continued, he spoke softly, almost whispering, as though he were sharing a deep secret with a close confidante. "Of course, we do have our special arrangements, don't we? Nothing out of the ordinary, nothing illegal, and certainly nothing to raise any deep concerns. As you know, I make sure we always do everything according to department policies and procedures."

Mr. Reed knew very well that the district supervisor of construction, his assistant, and two previous commerce officers had taken bribes. The special arrangement he mentioned concerned the awarding of contracts without tendering, using the specious argument that a contractor offered 'superior' products or services, even though this could never be properly shown.

Rager knew of the practice because his predecessor had advised him to take bribes from the Mensen Air Charter Services Company, which provided the air service to the Indian Affairs tourist camps. The official had told him, "Teddy Mensen gives you a two-week, fully paid holiday on Paradise Island in the Bahamas if you give him the contract. All you have to do is write a memo to file that says he is the only airline that understands the operation and meets our needs – the type of aircraft, for example – and no one needs to be the wiser." The owner of the company, a big blustery Dutchman, had shown up in the office expecting Rager to extend the contract, but Rager had flatly refused and said he would tender the contract. "I'd like to get a few competitive bids before awarding the contract. Let's see who offers the lowest bid. You should know, too, that I don't take bribes. I never have and never will."

Mr. Reed knew all this because the owner, Teddy Mensen, had phoned him to complain. "I don't like your new commerce officer, not one bit," he said. "I don't want to lose the contract."

"Just wait; we'll get him on side," Mr. Reed advised.

But now Mr. Reed pretended not to know anything. "We also have audits, don't we?" he said. "If any district official was taking a bribe, I would certainly know about it."

This, too, was a fabrication. Mr. Reed knew that audits were undertaken only every three or four years, and when they were, district files often went missing – torn up or burned in the town dump – while he himself played golf, napped, delegated authority, read flimsies, and avoided travelling to the villages as much as possible. Mr. Reed had a terrible fear of flying, especially in small floatplanes, the ones that flew to the Indian villages. So great was his fear of flying that he drove twelve hundred kilometers one way and the same return distance – a trip that should have taken two days took a full week, and in the winter often two weeks – rather than flying from Thunder Bay to Toronto to meet the regional director general.

All in all, Mr. Reed was a terrible liar. Rager went along with the façade knowing the agency had little concern for what happened in the Nakina district. Why else would they keep a district manager who was an incompetent fool, a liar, and a man afraid to fly?

But Mr. Reed was not quite finished with undermining Sister Brunelle's accusations. "I don't know where she gets her population figures!" he declared. "She writes that, according to parish records, Windsor House has two hundred and two Indians. I would think the number would be much smaller, what with half the original population having left to form Big Beaver House, and of those who stayed, why, a number might have moved to an outpost camp. God knows the Indians in the villages live like Gypsies – moving around; here today and gone tomorrow. A strange race, if you ask me. They even pop up here in Grayson looking for work, and there is none."

It was difficult to know the precise resident population in any of the district villages. Families often moved to a town or city in search of employment or a higher standard of living before returning to the village disappointed. At other times they moved to a traditional outpost camp, looking for something they had lost long ago and hoped to reclaim. There were the unrecorded births and deaths that no one seemed to know anything about, least of all Indian Affairs. People were born and people died, and only the elders seemed to know who they were. Because of these problems, the district office never knew the precise population size of any of the villages. They could only rely on what a band administrator told them, which raised another concern. Since the agency determined the level of funding a village received based on population size, there was always an incentive for a band administrator to inflate the population number. As a consequence, agency officials adjusted the population number downward. And so, it was a great fiction: band administrators providing one figure and district officials using another.

In the end, it made no difference. The district officials did as they always did: they increased or decreased the population size to fit the budget. They made the numbers work.

"But she could be right – two hundred and two Indians could be the correct number?"

"Yes – she could be right," Rager said.

"We don't really know, do we? "

"No, we don't."

"She mentioned the parish records. Would that take into account the Anglicans who left?" Mr. Reed answered his own question. "I guess we don't really know, do we, after all why would the Catholic mission track the number of Anglicans?"

"No, we don't know,"

"Do you think she did a head count?" Mr. Reed asked.

"If I had been in Windsor House for six months," Rager replied, "I would have done a head count. All you have to do is visit each of the households, ask those present how many people live in the house, repeat the exercise a couple of times, and establish a trend line. Another way would be to work with the elders, ask them what they do know: how many people live in a household, if they leave the village where do they go, the number of unrecorded births and deaths, and so on.

"The elders know everything. They're like walking encyclopedias; you just need to ask them and listen. Often, too, there's one very smart informant, it could be a man or a woman, who knows just about everything that's happening in a village. You just have to find that one person, gain their trust, and ask them the right questions. It could even be a priest, like Father Benoît, or a resident nurse. But you need to gain their trust. It's not as easy as it seems. Gaining anyone's trust is difficult – in my experience, it has to be earned."

Mr. Reed seemed annoyed with Rager's reply. "Yes, certainly. Trust needs to be earned, thank you," he spoke curtly. He stared up at the ceiling. He could hear the rain beginning to fall. The distant and heavy pounding was comforting, like the sound of a drum in the distance. He would go home soon, eat a proper meal that Mrs. Reed – Janet – had prepared. After supper, they would watch television – *All in The Family* was a favourite show. It would be another pleasant evening. He only needed to get through this meeting with the younger man, the man he knew so little about and cared for not a whit.

He turned his attention away from the ceiling; it was soothing, but boring. "Well, I think I know what we need to do. We need an action plan. I think that would be appropriate. Something with progressive projects, but nothing special or radical, nothing with a great deal of cost. No, whatever we do, we must stay within the district budget or gain regional approval for additional funding. Do you have any suggestions?"

Rager stared at the older man. Mr. Reed's deceit and ability to pretend he knew nothing about bribes or the reality of the village was outstanding. A simple walk through Windsor House revealed everything: empty, moldy houses, vacant buildings, beaten-down faces, and the smell of defeat.

When Rager spoke, he kept his hands clasped in the form of a silent prayer. "I haven't been to Windsor House, except once. Nonetheless, I know there's a lot we can do. We own and operate sixteen tourist camps; two of them are on the Attawapiskat River near Windsor House and two others on nearby lakes. I know the villagers rely on the seasonal work that the camps generate, serving as fishing guides, cooks, and camp attendants. One of the guides is a man named William Suganaqueb. When I met him, he seemed to be a decent man, hardworking and knowledgeable. I doubt he's a drunk." He described two other local fishing guides, not that he knew much about any of the men. What could anyone know after a thirty-minute conversation?

Unlike the district manager, Rager enjoyed flying in floatplanes and spending time in Indian villages. In his three years as a business advisor with the Ontario Cooperative Development Association he had often worked with Indian store managers, advising them on pricing, investing, store expansion, and travelling to Winnipeg with them to negotiate favourable wholesale food rates. After days in the villages, he would often go out hunting and fishing. He felt that the Nakina district was no different.

"I've met with Father Benoît," he said. "Sister Brunelle is correct. Father Benoît has a heart condition. He sees a cardiologist in Ottawa on a regular basis. I expect he'll be leaving Windsor House soon. His assistant, Brother André, is almost totally deaf and can barely hear anything you say. He keeps asking you to repeat yourself. I expect that he, too, will be leaving the village. I know the band administrator, Luke Atlookin, although not very well. My first impression is that he's intelligent but not to be trusted."

Rager suggested a number of projects to revitalize the local village economy. "We could subsidize the portable sawmill seasonally and use the lumber to build and repair houses. It would provide employment and improve the housing stock. We could use the lumber to build and repair the tourist camps – the camps are in poor condition. We could also invest in modernizing the camps, adding saunas, two-way radios, new furniture, and appliances. There are other nearby lakes where I'm told the fishing is spectacular and we could build more tourist camps on those lakes. With the right sort of modern camps offering spectacular fishing, we could increase employment and income for the village.

"In my introductory circuit to the fly-in villages, all the chiefs and councils said they wanted to start a development corporation to own and operate the camps. I think that is something we should support. After all, why is the government in the business of owning and operating sports fishing camps when it should be the villages? We could start by doing a business plan for the development corporation; it would help confirm markets, ownership structure, and required capital investment. I think those are the projects I would focus on starting in Windsor House. Think of it. Over a number of years, the village could pull itself out of its misery. At the very least, it would be a good start.

"I can't think of anything else, not off the top of my head – oh, we should repair and re-open the school. Why would anyone stay in Windsor House without a school? Keeping it closed for whatever reason seems to me to be cruel and negligent."

Mr. Reed had followed the advice of the district supervisor of schools in closing the school. He had never given his decision a second thought.

"Thank you for those suggestions, but we must never rush," Mr. Reed said. "No, we must never rush: we need to be careful. Still, we need to do something, or at the very least appear to be doing something. Stewart will expect it – I know he will."

He looked at the nun's letter more carefully; the crucifix on the mast head was worrisome. It seemed as though a watchful god was waiting for him to act. "I expect that Stewart will phone me soon, possibly even today." The regional officials in Toronto loved nothing better than to make the district officials squirm. The regional director general operated in much the same fashion. He could make Mr. Reed squirm with a simple phone call.

"John," he said to Rager, finally, "I'd like you to visit Windsor House as soon as possible. Meet with the chief and council, offer up some of your ideas about opening the sawmill, repairing houses, and building more tourist camps. See what they say. Of course, it could be any sort of project, anything at all, even a small arts and crafts kiosk selling trinkets to the sports fishermen – watch bracelets, earrings, hair clips, all that sort of thing. Just don't make any promises. We can't really promise anyone anything, not until we get funding approval. Region controls the purse strings. Oh, I almost forgot. I suppose we should repair and reopen the school. A year is a long time to keep children out of school."

Rager unclasped his hands and politely smiled. "Why don't we include the five fly-in villages in a project to start their own development corporation and take over the ownership of the agency camps? Windsor House would be one of the owners. We could tell region it's a pilot project."

"Not a bad idea, but we have to be careful. We don't want to raise any expectations, not until we get approval. Let's not get ahead of ourselves, sir." Mr. Reed handed Rager the file with the nun's letter. It was the end of their meeting.

The district manager left early, well before anyone else. By five thirty, Rager was alone in the office, a lonely figure working in a back office crowded with files. At eight o'clock, he left.

As he walked back to the rooming house, he thought of Windsor House; so far away, so isolated, with a broken and neglected people. What did he really know of the village? A man who had only been in the village once for three days, a man who lived alone in a rooming house was akin to a man adrift at sea on a raft, with the great tides moving

him. He was a form of human flotsam with no thought of when or how it might end. And yet, he could feel the pull, the steady pull of greater forces. But to what end, and to what purpose? He thought of the nun's words in the letter. "I ask you to remember that they are your brothers and sisters and I ask you to act in good conscience." *We belong to one another,* Rager thought – and for a moment, it seemed to be the only truth that really mattered.

Chapter 3
A STRANGE INHUMAN SCREAM

(1)

During his three years working for the Ontario Cooperative Development Association, Rager lived with Helen and Sam in a cramped, two-bedroom Sioux Lookout apartment. After Helen left, he felt a sense of relief for a time, as though a heavy weight had been lifted off his shoulders. It was only much later that he felt regret.

By the end of his last year with OCDA, the manager asked him to take on a very different project. "I would like you to go to a small town not far from Kenora named Bristol. There are a number of non-status Indians who live outside Bristol in a shantytown. They lost their treaty status when one of their maternal ancestors married a non-Indian. What they need is government housing, not shacks, and the Grand Chief of Treaty Three requested that we send someone to help them. What I would like you to do is go to Bristol, rent a cabin, and help the people apply for government housing. You'll have to research the available government housing programs. I would think there is some sort of program they would be eligible to apply under. After that, you hustle back here and continue your other work."

This was the background to the day that he found himself walking with a young Indian woman named Elena Ottertail from the Treaty Three office along a rail line to the shantytown, eight kilometers outside Bristol, the two of them lonely soldiers on an impossible mission. At one point he asked Elena if the people had tried to get help from either level of government. "So far, not much luck" she said.

"Is that why they built the shantytown?"

"Yes, they had no choice. A few years back, they lived in an outpost camp north of Bristol. This was before Indian Affairs officials showed up and told them they had to send their children to residential school, otherwise Children's Aid would place them in foster care. No one wanted to send their children to residential school, knowing how badly the schools treated Indian children. On the other hand, they certainly didn't want their children put in foster care. When the people asked Indian Affairs to build them a school, the officials refused because they were non-status. When they appealed to the provincial government for a school, they were told they were Indians, and therefore not a provincial responsibility. In so many words, they found themselves in a no-man's land where the two levels of government play ping-pong with definitions and people's lives. So, they moved to Bristol, hoping to rent houses." Elena paused before adding, "But no one in Bristol wanted to rent them houses or cabins. All they saw were a bunch of Indians with no money and no full-time jobs. Residents thought they would lower property values. So, they had no choice but to build a shantytown and send their children to school in Bristol."

There was very little to Bristol except a general store, church, primary school, gas station, train station, two seasonal tackle shops, and houses and cabins. What made the town unique was its location as the gateway to a region of lakes, abundant wildlife, and spectacular sports fishing. There was also the Bristol Lodge. The Canadian National Railroad had built the lodge at the turn of the century; it was a massive structure with a hundred guest rooms, marble bathrooms, and a great dining room in addition to four tennis courts, a nine-hole golf course, and a marina with motorboats, speedboats, cedar canoes, fan boats, and floatplanes. There were also the cottages on the lakes – some were simple family hideaways while others were luxury cottages with saunas, guest houses, and every imaginable toy. The small town was the center of a boreal wilderness paradise.

It was a long walk. At one point, Rager asked, "I would think it's hard on the children, walking like this every day?"

"It is," Elena replied. "Every day for ten months of the year, the children – some as young as six or seven – walk to school, back and forth. That's a six-mile walk one-way, twice a day. There are also the trains that travel along the rail line, which are a danger. You'll see that when we come to a trestle, a hundred yards long, that spans over a steep canyon. Whenever a fast-moving train comes along, the children have to run for their lives. But that's not all. In the winter when it's cold or there's a snowstorm and the children don't go to school, the authorities threaten the parents. They say, 'Your children have to go to school or we'll take them away and place them in foster care,' and sometimes they do. Children's Aid sweeps down and takes the children. When the parents turn to the courts, the government lawyers always win.

"When you think about it, the government is the *real* problem. They tell them their children have to go to school, but make it impossible by denying them a school where they once lived or providing housing in a town with a school, at least up to now."

"Are you related to the families?" Rager asked.

"Yes," she answered. "It's cruel, what the government does."

After an hour, they turned off the rail line and entered thick bush. They followed a path through a gulley until they came to an open place, where Rager could see a dozen shacks. The stench of human waste permeated the air. An elder stoked a slow-burning fire as clouds of black flies droned everywhere. With his long, grey, wispy hair, dark and wrinkled face, missing teeth, and knotted hands, the elder could easily have been a mythical figure in a Japanese Noh play. He hardly paid any attention to his two visitors, except to give Elena a nod. Nearby, children played in a clearing: a girl with a broken doll, a waif-like boy pulling a choo-choo train, and a dozen or so older children attempting to build a shack out of branches and cardboard. It could easily have been a Calcutta slum – all that was missing was a Hindu priest chanting over a corpse.

Elena spoke with the elder. She explained that Rager had been sent to help them apply for government housing. She asked his permission to walk through the shacks so Rager could see for himself their living conditions. "He has to see how you live with his own eyes," she said.

"Yes, go, look," the elder replied.

They walked through the shacks, where he saw mud floors, foam mattresses, clothes crammed into cardboard boxes, cold pots of food sitting over Coleman stoves, and the sad posters hanging on walls: Marilyn Monroe standing over a crate in a billowing dress, the Virgin Mary cradling Christ in her arms, and the Archangel Michael leading a host of angels. When they came out, they spoke. "Where are you from?" the elder asked.

"Sioux Lookout, but I grew up in Montreal," Rager replied.

The man's face lit up. "I know Montreal, I know it well. I've walked on Mount Royal. I've stood on the lookout. I've seen the buildings and the bright city lights. I remember Saint Joseph's Oratory, with its huge basilica and the steps where the pilgrims climb on their knees while they do their rosaries. I remember the downtown – Saint Catherine, Saint Lawrence, Saint Denis, Stanley, and Peel streets. I remember all the bars and restaurants, the Esquire Show Bar, and the strip joints on Saint Lawrence – the Main.

"You see, I lived in that city for four years, from 1952 to 1956, and for a year I lived with an Italian woman named Francesca Rosa. She was a beautiful young woman, with long black raven hair, fierce eyes like Sophia Loren, and a body that makes a man's knees shake. She was twenty-three, and I was this crazy, wild Indian with his hair in braids who wore a buckskin jacket. I was thirty-one.

"The first time I saw her," he said, "she was standing on a crowded downtown bus. We both noticed each other. I guess it was unavoidable. We were both exotic, different, and stood out from the crowd. When she got off the bus, I followed her two blocks, tapped her on the shoulder, and said 'Miss, you forgot something.'

"'What?' she asked.

"'Me!'

"She laughed. After that we went for coffee. I told her I was an Apache Indian from Arizona exploring the country and she believed me. I guess she wanted to believe that this wild Indian was crazy about her. We lived together in an apartment near Atwater, not far from the Montreal Forum, until she left me for an Italian contractor. I suppose from her point of view, I was not the marrying kind. I don't blame her. But we had fun together for almost a year."

The elder stood for a moment without speaking. He began to reminisce. "There wasn't anything we wouldn't do together. We went to nightclubs, hung out with all sorts of people, even the strippers and pimps, it didn't matter, everyone came to our apartment. Once, we drove up to the Laurentian Mountains to stay at an inn. I even went downhill skiing. Imagine this crazy Indian in a buckskin jacket skiing down a hill! In those days I worked as a deckhand on the lakers. I travelled up and down the St. Lawrence River and all over the Great Lakes, with

Montreal as my home base. It was a crazy life, a wild ride. I wouldn't trade it for anything."

He poked the embers of the fire. "You know, people often forget the past," he said. "The St. Lawrence River flows all the way to the Atlantic Ocean. In Canada, it's the great artery that connects the Great Lakes to the rest of the world.

"I suppose you know the story of the voyageurs – how they always started their long canoe trips from Lachine, Quebec, and canoed up into the Ottawa River, then along the Great Lakes before they reached Old Fort William, the 'Great Rendezvous.' It was there that the Indians, Metis, French, and English came together to trade. The Indians traded their furs for cloth, guns, bullets, and other supplies, and the traders for the furs, which they took back to Montreal, loaded onto ships, and sent across the ocean to Europe. Imagine all those fur pelts travelling thousands of kilometers, just so some rich people in Europe could parade around in beaver hats and fur coats! That was a long time ago, and things have changed." As the elder spoke, his eyes shined as though he were staring into an eternity where every thought, every image, every action had brought him here, to where he lived in a shantytown. "Will you help us?" he asked.

"Yes," Rager replied.

"Good."

(2)

In the days that followed, Rager researched to see if there were any government housing programs for the very poor.

He settled on a new provincial housing program through which a group of people could form a non-profit housing association and apply for funding to offset the cost of purchasing the land, architectural services, building materials, and electrical and plumbing contractors, while using their own "sweat equity" to construct the houses.

He arranged to meet with four of the men who lived in the shantytown to explain the program. "You have to form a housing association to be eligible," he said. "But I can arrange to hire a lawyer and Ontario Cooperative Development Association will pay the cost."

Rager outlined the risks and benefits. "There is no guarantee that the government will approve your application, but there is no other program. You also have to contribute your own labour to build the houses, but I think you can do that if the houses are kept modest. It will certainly be better housing than what you have. You also won't have the problem of your children having to walk a long distance to school every day, or the threat of Children's Aid hanging over your heads." All the men agreed with Rager. When it came to supplying their own labour, one of them spoke for the group: "There isn't one of us who can't hold a hammer and nails."

Rager hired a lawyer to incorporate the housing association; filled out the program application forms, which the men signed; submitted the forms; and lobbied politicians to support the application – the local Member of the Ontario Legislative Assembly, the Member of Parliament, and the local reeve. He wrote letters to government officials, advising them, "There are sixteen adults and twenty children who live in shacks eight kilometers outside of Bristol. The children walk to school every day. A number of families have lost their children who are now in foster care because of poor school attendance. The need for housing is grave. Without housing, they are in danger of losing all their children. If your agency can provide funding for six modest houses, it will keep families together, it will save lives." Rager wrote and harassed anyone that had anything to do with approving the application to the point that they stopped taking his phone calls.

Within three weeks, an official named Roger Holiday wrote back, denying their application. He listed a number of reasons: the applicants were unemployed, depended on welfare, did not have bank accounts, and offered no guarantee that they would maintain the houses properly. He insinuated that they only knew squalor and would destroy new houses. Notwithstanding the appeal of the Treaty Three Grand Chief, their application was rejected a second time. Rager later discovered that all it took was a phone call from one of the lodge owners to have the application rejected.

(3)

On an August evening when the wind was warm and soft, the Ontario premier came to Bristol. The gentleman – a lawyer with grey hair, a smooth, tanned face, and a perpetual look of calm and determination – arrived on a blue government de Havilland twin-engine Otter floatplane that seemed to float down from the sky onto the lake like a visiting spaceship. When the premier stepped ashore and walked into the lodge, the assembled crowd clapped spontaneously. He was one of them. They could feel his pride and love, and they knew him as he did them.

The lodge was magnificent. It seemed to glow, a strange sight as the sun came down onto the golf course. The crowd that gathered watched the premier shaking hands – their hands – and the waiters in the dining room passed around drinks. A five-piece band had set themselves up and the music drifted everywhere. Couples who rarely danced began to dance spontaneously. In attendance were elected officials, tourism operators, business people from outside Bristol, and reeves and mayors from nearby towns. "Maybe our own businesses can get a government contribution" was the prevailing sentiment.

When the premier spoke in the dining room about the benefits of a ski hill to the region and the prospect of starting a winter tourism industry, he was given more applause. Rager sat in the back, disgusted with the spectacle as much as himself.

He eventually retreated to a municipal park, where he stood on a dock surrounded by motorboats and sailboats. He looked out across the lake to the glittering lights above the lodge and felt terrible. There was nothing left to do but leave Bristol. Just then, a badly beaten man from the shantytown, one of the four men he originally met, appeared on the dock. "Who beat you up, Walter?" Rager asked.

"My son," he replied.

"Why?"

"He's angry with me."

"Why is he angry with you?"

"Because we moved here."

"You had no choice," Rager commented.

"It doesn't matter, he doesn't understand. I don't know what to do. We applied for housing like you asked us to, and nothing came of it. No one cares – not a goddam soul!"

"I care."

"John, you have no power, you have no knowledge of government, and you create false hope. Which is worse, no hope or false hope? Go back to Sioux Lookout – just go. This is the end for us. We have nothing left except each other, and now even that is falling apart. You understand? We're finished, we're done."

Walter walked away without saying another word.

An hour had passed when a middle-aged woman from the shantytown appeared. Rager knew her as Cathy. "I'm so very tired, so very weak, I don't know if I can walk back along the rail line tonight," she said. "Sometimes I just want to lie down on the tracks and let the train run me over. I would never know what happened. Do you have anything to drink – tell me you do, please, honey?" She brushed his hand.

"I have nothing to drink, Cathy."

"Nothing to drink, so sad. How about weed?"

"No – I have no weed."

"How about a cigarette?"

"I don't smoke. Why not go to the lodge? There's lots to drink and it's free."

"I've already tried. They told me to go away. They made me feel like a beaten dog. Do you think the government is trying to kill us?"

"I hope not."

The woman was a bag of bones, a stick-like creature. They sat down together. She told him that her husband was dead and her children had been placed in foster care. "They called me a bad mother. Do you think I'm bad?"

"No, Cathy, you're not bad. You just got caught up in forces you have no control over. It's the government officials who don't care. They pretend they do, and like the politicians, they only care for themselves."

"I have no reason to live – not anymore," she said. "I don't care if I die; it would be better."

"I wish I could have done more, Cathy. Forgive me for failing. Please, forgive me?"

"You're a good man, but you don't know anything. The government has been doing this to us for a long time."

"I guess I know that now."

The woman walked away, leaving him alone on the dock. Rager moved into the park. He lay down on the ground. It was warm. He imagined that he could feel the enormous hidden forces, the molten mass of heat, that lay below. "I can't do anything for these people," he thought. "They have no purpose, no value, and the government treats them like dirt. Nothing will ever change that fact. I might move to another town, another city, another country, but it will never change the reality that no one cares what happens to these people."

All through the night he kept on thinking of the shantytown. Where might the people go? It would likely be Winnipeg. He imagined a dark-brick tenement building, a city park, people sleeping on benches, and a scream in the night – a strange, inhuman scream, as though someone were being beaten to death. Then he fell into a deep sleep.

When he woke, the sun was burning through the early morning fog; a strange, living, moving fog that crept over the water before finally running away. When the sun appeared, he watched sail boats passing by, full of men and women gaily laughing. He even saw the premier with a female assistant board the Otter and fly away. It seemed to be a dream – an illusion – and a great jest!

In the months that followed, Rager applied for the position of Indian Affairs Nakina District Commerce Officer and the agency hired him without ever holding an in-person interview. "You were the only one who applied," the regional superintendent of economic development told him.

Someone once told Rager, "The government is us, you know. We elect our members of parliament and they represent us: in a way, they are us." But Rager knew differently. The government was an organization run by men with funny names like Roger Holiday. He wanted to know more about these men. Why were they so mean – was it simply power? He also wanted to redeem himself. Why not take a risk – what could he lose?

His decision to accept the position brought him to Grayson, the rooming house, and Mr. Reed.

Chapter 4
AN AMBITIOUS MAN

(1);

From mid-August to early September, severe thunderstorms swept through the region with a terrible vengeance. Rain poured down, drowning lakes and rivers, and tornado winds tore through forests leaving deep scars. In some of the low-lying Indian villages, there was heavy flooding. For most of a three-week period, the floatplanes were grounded and flights were cancelled. The impact on the air charter companies and sport fishing operators meant a loss of revenue in an industry that relied heavily on a short four-month season to generate most of its annual revenues. For the flooded Indian villages, the storms meant evacuation to towns and cities. It was also punishing on the gravel roads, especially the road between Grayson and Nakina. And then suddenly the storms stopped and life returned to normal.

Not long after the bad weather had passed, Rager and the district supervisor of local government, Gordon Hughes, drove together in the agency station wagon to the Mensen float base two kilometers outside Nakina. Both men were flying to fly-in villages and were scheduled to depart at precisely one o'clock. Rager would fly to Windsor House to consult with the chief, council, and as many villagers as possible on what they saw as priorities for an action plan. Gordon Hughes would fly to Fort Moore to meet with the chief and council on the number of houses allocated to the village for the next fiscal year.

But the gravel road was a maze of potholes, crisscrossing ruts, and mounds of gravel waiting to be graded. It was, therefore, difficult for Rager to drive at a decent speed. Given the road conditions, they would almost certainly be late. More challenging was that every time Rager steered in one direction, the station wagon pulled in the opposite. "Why would anyone buy such a terrible car?" he wondered. It was Mr. Reed who had selected the station wagon for its size and comfort, not its steering.

They had been on the road less than fifteen minutes when a slow-moving grader suddenly appeared, blocking the road ahead. After a few minutes, Rager honked, hoping the operator would pull to the side and let them pass. But the operator paid no heed. Rager honked again. Still no response. At that point, Gordon rolled down the side window and began to yell. "MOVE OUT OF THE WAY, ASSHOLE! MOVE THE FUCKING GRADER!" He continued yelling until his face turned a deep beet red with white blotches and contorted like a man on the verge of having a stroke.

After a few minutes, Gordon stopped and accepted what seemed to be inevitable, "You know, we're going to miss our plane!" he said. "No doubt about it, we're fucked royally!" He lit a cigarette, took a deep drag, and hesitated before exhaling. The long stream of smoke filled the car's interior like filthy smog.

"Gordon, relax," Rager counselled. "Mensen will wait. He's not going to let one of his planes leave without us; money is too important to him."

His comforting words meant nothing to the supervisor, who was impatient to get the trip over and done with. Gordon wondered why he was going to Fort Moore to meet the chief and council in the first place when he could have easily mailed the Band Council Resolution for signatures. In fact, the trip was more of a formality than anything else; regional office had already made the decision to build two houses for the band in the 1976-77 fiscal year and not the promised eight. "Sometimes you win and sometimes you lose, and that's life. You don't always get what you want," he thought. There was nothing the chief and council could do but accept the decision. They would complain of course, as they always did, like spoiled and coddled children, but it would be useless. Besides, it was not up to them to set budgets. It was up to the agency – and more importantly, those who sat in Toronto regional office and Ottawa headquarters.

Gordon was still not happy with the grader, however. "That idiot driving the grader should know better," he said. "He's a fucking asshole, a real fucking asshole! He should move over. Just fucking move over, mister!" He squeezed his hand into a hard ball. For a moment it seemed he might roll down the window and start yelling all over again, or possibly jump out of the car, run up to the grader, and punch the driver in the face. But he did no such thing. He glared, smoked, butted out his cigarette, lit another, smoked harder, mumbled, and pretended he was a man of great importance on an important mission with very little time to waste. Why should he have to endure a fool's behavior – why indeed?

Gordon Hughes was a short, squat Welshman in his late thirties, and a former Hudson's Bay store manager accustomed to having his own way. He had been with "The Bay" for eighteen years before joining Indian Affairs two years earlier. As a district supervisor of local government, his responsibility was to advise the nine chiefs and councils on all matters related to governance, including holding elections, passing by-laws, hiring a band manager, communicating with band members, and planning and monitoring delivery of programs and services. Yelling and screaming like he did was simply a matter of letting everyone know that he was a man of action, not one to be toyed with. For that very reason, he fully expected to replace Mr. Reed when the district manager retired.

At one point the supervisor asked Rager matter-of-factly, "Do you agree that the operator should move?"

"Not really. He may know something we don't," Rager replied. "It could be a lot worse up ahead. Maybe there's been an accident, maybe the road has collapsed somewhere, how do we know? Well, we don't, do we?"

"I doubt there's been an accident or the road's collapsed. The operator's just a fucking asshole, a complete fucking asshole, a turd, if you don't mind. I don't know what else to call him – maybe a cunt!" After Gordon spoke, his face cooled down, the steam slowly leaving the pot, and he began to stretch his words as though he were trying to make amends for being vulgar. "I don't mean to offend, but the man is a complete and utter fool. He has no right to hold us up – none whatsoever. Quite simply," and here he couldn't help himself, "he's an asshole!"

"Thank you."

"You're welcome."

And that was the end of their brief exchange. They would have to drive behind the grader, moving at a crawl until they were given the signal to pass.

The supervisor was a difficult man to comprehend or have any sympathy for. He was rough; his hands were thick and calloused from years of lifting and moving heavy boxes, crates, oil drums, fur pelts, and everything else imaginable, on and off planes, into and out of Hudson Bay warehouses in remote villages. His mouth was wide, his lips were thin and grim, and his eyes were perpetually searching for another's weakness. And he reeked of nicotine – every time he spoke the smell lingered like bad gas. But he never seemed to notice, or care, that he was not a pleasant sight. His main thought was to reduce government spending and to think of ways in which that might be accomplished. "We need to control spending and cut back on expectations," was his favourite mantra, and he repeated it as though he were singing the same chant in a Hare Krishna temple until the words meant nothing and all thought and reason were gone. All in all, he was not a man to be trifled with on matters to do with budgets or government decision-making. In fact, he was ruthless, uncompromising, and mean.

After a few more minutes, Gordon spoke again. "I hate these trips. When you think about it, they really are rather useless."

"Useless?" Rager asked.

"Oh, I mean everything. Everything...and, I suppose, nothing." Gordon lit another cigarette, inhaled, and let out a long stream of smoke. As he did, Rager rolled down the window to let out some of the smoke that now engulfed the small space. It had little effect; the car continued to fill with smoke from a man who gave no thought to others. The supervisor stared out the side widow and gathered his thoughts.

Mr. Reed had hired Gordon, convinced that a Hudson's Bay store manager with years of work experience in remote Indian villages would bring a unique perspective to the district. But Mr. Reed had been wrong. Gordon knew very little about Indigenous culture and history. He could hardly tell the difference between a Mohawk, Ojibwa, Cree, Haida, Blood, Blackfoot, or any other Indigenous group. In his mind they were all spoiled and coddled Indians who were lucky to have the federal government meeting all their needs. Gordon thought the coddling would have to change. Yes, indeed it would have to change, and it must change.

On more than one occasion, Gordon wondered why the villages could not be reduced in number to reduce costs. He brought it up one day with Mr. Reed as they were sitting together pondering the future. "Why can't we have two large villages instead of nine small district villages – say, one large village in the south, on Highway 11, and one in the north?"

Mr. Reed thought about how this would reduce his need to travel and readily agreed. "Of course," Gordon continued, "the chiefs and councils will complain. They always do. But it's not their decision to make. We make the decisions, not them. I mean, the federal government decides on how best to spend tax-payer dollars, not any chiefs or councils with a vested interest to waste money."

But neither man ever said any of this to anyone in the Toronto regional office because they knew it was far too political. They mentioned the idea to a couple of the other district supervisors, who agreed the idea had merit.

As Gordon and Rager crawled toward Nakina in the station wagon, the Welshman mentioned the idea of reducing the number of villages. In no uncertain terms, the new commerce officer replied, "Who ever gave you the idea that you or anyone else in government could close down villages willy-nilly? You sound like an arrogant fool!"

"I don't like your tone, John."

"Well," Rager replied, "I don't like what you're saying, so stop it."

But Gordon could not stop. As he thought along these lines, he again wondered why, in fact, he was travelling to Fort Moore in the first place. "Why am I going?" he thought. "It's absolutely ridiculous when you think about it. So, they live in crowded houses and need more houses, so what? The houses are free. Too bad. They'll have to wait until we decide what they get. Until then they can suck lemons. If they want to do something positive, they can just stop having babies." It was common knowledge that the villages were rapidly growing – 'babies having babies.' He wondered when it would end. Is the government supposed to hand out contraceptives?

Gordon envisioned a future with a great mass of industry – mines, pulp mills, sawmills, hydro stations, all-season roads, and rail lines – and a reduced number of Indian villages. In this utopian future he saw himself as a senior official in Ottawa, possibly a deputy minister – a portly man in his early sixties, slightly grey, his hair thinning with a bald spot, holding meetings with cabinet ministers to discuss how best to control spending on an ever-increasing Indian population. So lost in this ridiculous fantasy, all his sense of proportion was lost. He was a minor official with minimal education, no in-depth knowledge of government, and more importantly, he knew no one of any importance in Ottawa. But none of this entered his mind – not one little bit.

Halfway to Nakina, the grader operator signaled for them to pass. When he did, the gravel road was smooth. It seemed to Gordon to be a signal to sit back and speak his mind to someone he considered of no real importance, on what he would do when he became district manager.

"You should know that when I'm appointed district manager, I will introduce a number of changes. First off, I'll develop a district plan with clear goals and objectives and, of course, tighter budget controls. No more uncontrolled spending, absolutely none of that. I'll do it the way the Bay does it, the way they always did, with annual targets. For example, say the district supervisor of education saves money on schools, he gets a cash bonus. The same would apply to the other supervisors. Just think of it – housing, capital projects, education, social services, and economic development – all with targets to reduce spending. It only makes sense. How can we achieve cuts if we don't offer rewards?" He continued speaking without bothering once to ask if Rager had anything to say in reply.

"A dangerous fool!" is all Rager could think.

Chapter 5
A DESPERATE MAN

(1)

On the lake outside of Nakina, the floatplanes – De Havilland Otters, Beavers, Cessnas, and the occasional Norseman – were landing, taxiing, and flying off to the point that it almost seemed a repeat of early June when the lodges and outpost camps first opened. But it was September now. The sportfishing season was ending and the three air charter companies were simply doing their best to make up for the period of bad weather. At each of the float bases, sportfishermen crowded to board floatplanes, each hungry to reach a lodge or outpost camp.

On the mound overlooking the Mensen Company dock – the smallest of the three companies – the owner, Teddy Mensen, a tall Dutchman with a heavy, bloated stomach, thick, curly blond hair, and cold blue eyes, paced back and forth, constantly looking as though he were about to do something awful. Suddenly, without hesitation he walked down to the dock and reprimanded a dock boy for loading an Otter too slowly. "Put some muscle into your work or you'll be fired!" he said. Then he loaded a few boxes to show how the work should proceed and moved back to the mound. In his mind it was all necessary, even if one or two of the sportfishermen gave him a queasy look. He almost laughed out loud when he saw the look. "None of your business, Yank!" he thought. He did not like the Americans, not since the war. Nonetheless, they comprised the bulk of his customers, so he smiled and waved as though nothing had transpired.

Mensen had a way of thinking that started back during the war years when he first saw German soldiers goose-stepping through his hometown in the Netherlands. The tall blond Waffen-SS troops demanded that people "Heil" when they marched by, with everyone standing in awe and fear. What intrigued Mensen was the terror they generated, and it led him to join as a member. He was certain the Germans would conquer the world and the Waffen-SS, the elite troops, would spearhead their conquest. As the war progressed, he had no trouble in loading prisoners onto train cars destined to Mauthausen and eventually to Auschwitz, Sobibor, and other death camps. But in 1944, after the Allied Normandy landing and the subsequent invasion of France, Belgian, Luxembourg, and the Netherlands, and the previous loss of Stalingrad and the growing triumph of Russia in the east, Mensen realized that the end was almost near for the Germans. And so, he deserted and reintegrated himself into the Dutch population. He told his parents he had made a terrible mistake and only joined the SS to protect his family, the people he loved most. But the truth was, when the German Wehrmacht began to lose the war, he began to fear for his life and his role in the war.

In all the years that followed, the air charter owner came to realize that no one can predict a man or a country's destiny. But the need to bully never left him. Even as a child he was different: greedy, covetous, bullying, willing to cheat if he could win, and as he grew older, always willing to betray others. With the SS it had been the Jews, Gypsies, homosexuals, disabled, and even a member of his own family – he turned an uncle over to the Gestapo for being a Jewish sympathizer. He was a frightening young man, tall and pale with piercing blue eyes that seemed to focus on hate. His two younger brothers could never understand why he joined the SS. This eventually led to his immigration to Canada, where he changed his name from Rotmensen to Mensen and begged his parents for a loan, which he never repaid. A teacher once said, "You know, Teddy, you have the coldest blue eyes in the world. You show no pity." Perhaps that was why, alone on the mound, pacing back at forth, he had no friends.

After all the bad weather, the Dutchman had a great deal to worry about. For a small air charter company with eighty percent of annual revenues generated from sportfishing, a loss of three weeks of revenues was a serious financial blow. Moreover, the new Nakina District Indian Affairs Commerce Officer had told him he would not extend his contract to service the sixteen Indian Affairs-owned tourist camps and planned to issue a Request for Proposals to a number of companies. It was a decision that would likely cost Mensen the contract. Over the years he had gone to great lengths to bribe previous commerce officers for the contract, providing cash, trips to the

Caribbean, and prostitutes. He had fully expected that the new commerce officer would fall into line, but for now it seemed not to be. All of this was brought to a climax when a week earlier the manager of the Royal Bank in Grayson called to say that the bank was concerned about Mensen's cash flow and his company loans were under review

There was also the matter of the ownership of the Indian Affairs tourist camps. Although in poor condition, the camps were situated on unspoiled sites – places dotted with reefs, babbling brooks, and deep clear waters – which offered some of the best sportfishing in the region. They were also on protected sites pending new government policies to address aboriginal land interest; until then no other operator could get a land use permit. It was, therefore, important to secure ownership of the camps. If he could somehow purchase the camps – modernize them, build more camps and lodges – he would become a major player in the sportfishing industry instead of staying a small, struggling operator with a high debt load and a very uncertain future. A major obstacle, however, was the desire on the part of the five fly-in chiefs and councils to form a development corporation, secure ownership of the camps, and essentially do exactly what he himself proposed. He had heard that the new commerce officer fully supported this effort. If the chiefs and councils were to gain ownership of the camps, not only would Mensen have lost the contract on the camps, but he would also face a new industry competitor: an Indian-owned corporation backed by the government, poised to modernize, expand, and steal customers. It was something the

Dutchman could not – and would not – allow. "Those camps should be mine – not some Indians," he thought. "I've worked all my life to build my business! What have they done? Nothing!"

On that bright sunny day, watching the American sportfishermen waiting to board a floatplane, he could only think one thought: "I hate that man, John Rager!"

(2)

At two o'clock, the Mensen Air Charter float base was dead quiet. There were no sportfishermen crowding the dock or dock boys loading planes, only a single-engine Otter tied to the dock, heavily loaded with cases of pop, candy, and potato chips, its pontoons sinking deep in the water. An older pilot sat beside the plane reading a paperback and smoking a rollie. He waited for three passengers: Rager, Gordon, and a federal nurse. He expected their arrival at any moment.

Teddy sat in a lawn chair he had placed on the mound. He was on his third beer of the day and gazed out onto the lake, where the competition was busy. The Northwest Air Services Company was the largest regional carrier in northwestern Ontario, and two of its floatplanes were lined up, ready to taxi. Without so much as a sigh, he watched each of the planes take to the air as two others landed. With an ever-expanding fleet of floatplanes, wheeled planes, helicopters, float and land bases, a terminal in Sudbury, another in Thunder Bay, and a warehouse in Toronto, the company serviced a number of markets besides sportfishing: logging companies, mineral exploration companies, provincial and federal agencies, medical travel, and with a scheduled air service to all the communities and Indian villages throughout the greater region an expanding freight, fuel and passenger service. A recent newspaper article described the owners – a family of Italians out of Timmins whose father had successfully started an air charter company with one floatplane and, over four decades, turned the company into the largest regional carrier and tourism operator in the region – as an example of risk-taking and entrepreneurship.

As Mensen watched the Northwest floatplanes flying and landing, he grew increasingly confused and could hardly think straight. He drank his beer quickly and returned to the cooler for another. When he returned and sat down, he felt small, pathetic, and frightened. If only the new commerce officer would disappear, all his problems would be solved.

Gordon and Rager arrived, parked, and walked into the company office. No sooner did they step into the office when Mrs. Mensen – Lottie, a short stocky woman – accosted the supervisor of local government about an outstanding agency payment.

"Gordon, you're just the man I've been waiting to see. Do you know how long we've been waiting for that government check?" she asked.

"No," he replied.

"Three months, still no check!"

"It's not my problem," he replied. When it suited him, Gordon could easily part with government.

"You know, Gordon, we have bills to pay. I told you the last time you were here that we don't like taking government travel warrants. Every time we do, we end up waiting months to get paid. Why? I have no idea. Let me put it to you this way: how would you like it if that was your paycheck? I don't think you would be too happy, would you?" Lottie stared at Gordon as though he was a thug.

Gordon yawned. "I'll see what I can do, Lottie, but no promises, I don't run the government."

"But you work for the government."

"I do, yes. I do indeed, but I don't deal with accounts payable. We have others who handle that sort of thing. But I promise you I will speak to Mr. Reed about it. Maybe he can do something, speed things up. I agree that three months is a bit long to wait."

"You said that the last time."

"I did?"

"Yes, you did, Gordon. Do you think I'm stupid?"

"No, of course not."

"As for Mr. Reed, all I ever hear is 'Mr. Reed, Mr. Reed,' but I never see Mr. Reed.

Does Mr. Reed really exist?"

"Yes, Mr. Reed exists. He's a man with white hair, rather distinguished-looking, dresses well, always wear's a nice suit, usually a grey suit."

Lottie shook her head in disgust. "I know you don't really care, Gordon."

Gordon paid the fares with a government travel warrant. "I'm only taking this because you're here and the plane is waiting," Lottie said, but there was bitterness in her voice.

On their way to the dock both men stopped to speak with the owner. Mensen looked at his wristwatch – it was an expensive Rolex that he was proud to display. It seemed to represent all his efforts to build a business, conveying the message, "I am successful and worthy of your envy."

"You know, gentlemen," he said. "You were supposed to leave here at one o'clock. It's passed two. Don't you think you're cutting it close? We might have gone without you." He crossed his long, fat, enormous legs, belched, and smiled.

"We got stuck behind a grader, Teddy. The asshole wouldn't let us pass," Gordon said.

He stared at Gordon, somewhat annoyed, before replying. "Forget it. You're here. We still have to wait for another passenger, a nurse going to Otter Falls, so it doesn't matter. I guess she has the same problem with graders." Mensen decided to change the subject and pointed to the cooler. "Help yourselves to a beer, gentlemen – they're in the cooler."

"We're on duty travel, no can drink," Gordon said. He seemed pleased with his show of discipline.

"You government people, always so serious. No one needs to know, I won't tell." The Dutchman made a sad clown face. All he needed was powder, lipstick, and a costume to complete the picture: a big oaf doing summersaults in a circus.

Neither Gordon nor Rager bothered to comment.

"Oh, go get your bags!" Teddy said.

They retrieved their bags and food supplies, took them down to the dock, and returned to the mound, where they stood with Mensen and watched the planes on the lake. The flow of planes taxiing, flying, and landing continued at a slow, reduced pace. After a few minutes of silence, Gordon commented, "The competition seems busy today. It's almost as though they own the sky."

Teddy was not happy with the comment and let it show. "Yes, they do good business," he said. He could have easily struck the supervisor for being impertinent, but then, this wasn't wartime, when he could strike a civilian with no concern.

"The weather looks good though," Gordon said.

"Yes, good weather, wonderful!"

Mensen stood up from the lawn chair. He towered over both men. Given his bulk, it was easy to imagine him standing on a train station and holding a submachine gun. "Gordon, I need to speak with your partner, alone. We have a private matter to discuss." He placed his arm around the supervisor's shoulder and led him to the office, where he left him in the care of a young, attractive receptionist who did everything but sit on his lap. Mensen returned to the mound. He began to speak with Rager.

"Let's be honest, John, those camps of yours are almost not worth having." He proceeded to list all the reasons. They were in poor condition. With old bunk beds, used outboard motors, broken docks, dented aluminum boats, and leaky roofs they were unlikely to attract many sportfishermen without new investment. The Indians who lived in the nearby villages used the camps in the off-season as trapping cabins, with no regard for proper maintenance. There were fewer and fewer bookings; this made back-to-back flights more difficult, which meant less profit.

When Mensen finished his list, he waved his beer in the air as though he were speaking to an invisible audience. "Does anybody hear me?" he asked. Then he added, "Mister, you need to do something – and I can help you."

"Before you say anything," Rager replied, "You should know that the chiefs and councils want to start a development corporation and take over the ownership of the camps. I plan to help them develop a business plan outlining how that will work. I expect that the agency will invest in the camps and address all the issues you raised."

"It's a bad idea, let me tell you why." Mensen went on a long discourse about Indians knowing nothing about business, tourism, and the air charter business. He said the only good thing they brought was their knowledge of guiding, working as camp attendants or cooks, and repairing engines. They were, he said, "unsuitable" for business – it was not part of their "culture." Then he said the Indian guides often stole the liquor that the sportfishermen brought into the camps and that white university students were preferable because they were honest, better looking, cleaner, and spoke good English. He had nothing good to say about an Indian development corporation and predicted it would fail. "They have nothing at stake – all you're doing is giving them something for free. If you sell me the camps, help me get loans and contributions, I can make the business grow."

Rager was not impressed – in fact he was disgusted – and let it show. "The tourism camps were built to create employment and income for the fly-in villagers, not white university students," he replied. "If the business grows and expands – and I think it will, because I believe the government will invest in making improvements – and if we hire managers to train people in business, the people will learn how to run and operate the business successfully. Right now, they have no incentive because the camps are government owned and operated, and the government, as we all know, is poor at running businesses. If you owned the camps, the profits would go into your pocket, not into the villages. As for hiring Indians, what you're telling me is that you plan on replacing them with white university students.

"Let me say something else. The camps are on their traditional lands. If anyone has a right to own and benefit from the camps, it's the people who have lived on those lands for as long as anyone can remember, not some crook who bribes people for contracts, has no interest in anything but his own welfare, and couldn't care less what happens to the villages. Do you think for one moment that I'm crazy enough to agree with you? More to the point, how would the chiefs and councils respond if they saw you taking over when they have more rights than anyone to own those camps? I don't think they would be too happy. If the chiefs and councils want to form a development corporation and take over the camps, let me assure you that I will do everything in my power to see that it happens."

Without saying another word, the Dutchman reached over and placed his powerful right hand around the smaller man's neck and began to squeeze – gently at first, like a snake, but then with more force. When he did, he peered into the smaller man's eyes and spoke firmly. "Mister, you need to fix those camps. Maybe something bad is going to happen. You never know. Someone might get hurt."

In one swift motion, Rager pushed his hand away. "Fuck off!" he said. "Don't try to bully me. It won't work. By the way, I don't think you're ever going to have another contract from us."

Mensen stood back – seemingly taken by the man's outrage. "Don't be so sensitive," he said. "It's just me talking, nothing more, what's talk between friends?"

"I'm not your friend."

The Dutchman paused. He decided to take another tack. "John, I know so little about government. I know you try your best. I know there are reasons why the government doesn't invest in the camps – you have committees that have to give their approval, people to consult, reports to write, and important people to give their approval. I'm only giving you good advice. The camps are in poor condition. That makes us all look bad, it hurts everyone, and fewer customers mean less work for the Indians. I tell you like a true friend you should sell me the camps. I would make them work. Yes, I would hire more Indians. Yes, I would pay them good money – not seventy dollars a day like they get now, but a hundred dollars a day, sure, why not, keep the Indians happy, forget about the university boys."

"Of course, you would, Teddy, of course."

"So, you'll sell me the camps?"

"Not on my watch – never!"

The Dutchman carried his beliefs from the war like a fool carries an old worn-out piece of broken luggage. He spoke without thinking. "You know the Indians are like Jews," he said, "a subclass of people. You know as a white race we are superior and we have a duty, a responsibility, to keep our race pure."

"If you say so, Teddy."

"I say so – I *know* so. By the way, are you queer?" he asked out of the blue.

"No, I'm not queer. Are you?"

"If you said that to me during the war, you would be dead."

"Would I?"

"Yes, dead."

Rager was fed up with the offensive discussion. The owner was not only a thief and a bully, but a racist. "I find your talk offensive," he said. "I find you, in particular, disgusting. How you ever survived in business, I have no idea."

Mensen could no longer contain himself. With all his financial problems, he seemed to have reached a breaking point, and the slight man standing in front of him stood for all that was wrong. "You know," Mensen replied, "it was the Jews who started the First World War and then the Second, so they got what they deserved. Like the bible says, 'An eye for an eye, a tooth for a tooth.' A hundred million people died in the two wars, but only six million Jews. In my way of thinking, the Jews got off lightly. They're like lice you can't get rid of except with a gas oven."

"There seem to be a lot of people you don't like, Teddy."

Mensen paused, uncertain if he should continue, but then he did. "You know it was the Russians who won the war – not the Americans. Of course, there was the Jewish money, too." He decided to ask a question. "Did you ever read *Mein Kampf*?"

"No – I don't read junk."

"So, you know nothing about Adolf Hitler?"

"I know he was the man who killed millions of people, destroyed cities, butchered innocent men, women, and children, and gassed six million Jews."

"They deserved it," Mensen said. "Did you know that Roosevelt's Secretary of the Treasury, Morgenthau, was a Jew. The Jews control money everywhere. I heard that even the Northwest Company has Jewish investors. They corrupt everything. If Rommel had been given more German troops the war would have been different. The Americans never won the war; it was the Russians, backed with Jewish money, who won the war. Where do you think most Jews live? It's in the United States. A lot of them live in Canada, too. They run our cities, businesses, everything. You know they want to control the world, them and the communists."

"You believe that rubbish?"

"I do."

"Then you're a fool."

"Not as much of a fool as you."

How could Rager not have known? He looked at the Dutchman – the blond hair, the cold, piercing blue eyes, the bribes and the attempt at bullying. The look he gave the Dutchman let him know that Rager knew. What else was the man hiding – murder?

"I think you better leave now," Teddy said.

Rager left, somewhat shaken.

Just then, Mensen heard his wife calling. Her voice carried like an air raid siren – "TEDDY! TEDDY!" She came up to complain about a late food delivery. He told her to leave him alone. "I don't have time to talk about small stuff. You take care of it. Jesus, Lottie, phone another supplier." She was a fat cow, a stupid bitch, his children no better, and his business was falling apart. Mensen walked over to the cooler for another beer. He could almost strangle the commerce officer. Yes, strangling – murder – would be a good solution.

Rager and Gordon stood on the dock. They were quiet until a tall, bony woman appeared carrying a suitcase.

"I'm Clara Simpson," she said. "I'm the federal nurse in Otter Falls. Where might you gentlemen be travelling?"

"Fort Moore," Gordon said.

"Windsor House," Rager added.

"Oh my, I do hope it's not for long?"

"Two days, not very long," Rager replied.

"Oh, but still..."

"Not so good," Gordon commented.

The pilot briefed his three passengers on their flying time. "Depending on the wind, we'll reach Otter Falls in thirty minutes, drop off the cargo, Fort Moore in an hour, and Windsor House in two hours. We might pick up some passengers along the way. I never know until the last moment – we'll just have to wait and see."

"Locals?" the nurse asked.

"Yes, ma'am, locals."

They boarded the plane. There were only two seats in the cargo area. Gordon and the nurse took the seats, leaving Rager to take the co-pilot's seat. When the nurse saw all the cargo, she spoke out loud so everyone could hear. "You know all that candy and pop gives the locals diabetes and rots their children's teeth. The government should provide more subsidies for fruit and vegetables."

"And who, madam, is going to pay for those subsidies?" Gordon asked.

"Why, the government, of course."

"I see, the government pays. The next thing you know, you'll want the government to make selling candy a crime. Madam, we live in a free country and people can still do what they want. Do you want to make selling cigarettes a crime, too?"

"I have no idea what you're talking about. I'm not talking about cigarettes or anything else. I just wonder why we can't subsidize the transport of healthy, nutritious food? Why do people like you confuse the issue? You always do that sort of thing. What is wrong with you?"

A dock boy untied the plane and pushed it free from the dock. The pilot flicked the ignition switch and with a great roar the plane began to taxi. The pilot offered Rager a pair of mufflers to block out the noise. Soon they were airborne. At eight thousand feet the pilot leveled the plane on a steady course heading northeast. Rager rested his head against the side window. He began to feel a slow, swimming motion as the plane moved through an invisible sea. Everything was where it should be. The monster – the Nazi – was far below, drunk in a lawn chair.

Part Two

Chapter 1
THE VILLAGE

(1)

From the vantage point of a plane flying at eight thousand feet, the Ojibwa village was lost within the vast boreal wilderness, the "Blue Forest" – a region comprised as much by lakes, rivers, creeks, and bogs as by coniferous forest, bush, and eskers. And then, as though by a strange alchemy, Windsor House suddenly appeared: two small islands connected by a walkway in the middle of a lake, with a connecting river snaking its way to Hudson Bay. On the larger island – the "mainland" – were the houses, cabins, band office, Hudson's Bay Company store and warehouse, and the vacant houses and cabins that the Anglicans had abandoned four years earlier. Four inches above the ground were the numerous walkways that zig-zagged between houses and buildings. On a rainy day the ground turned into mush, making the walkways the only means of walking without being covered in mud. Almost everyone in the village lived on the mainland, except for the two clerics who lived on the smaller island. Emile Island was named after a dead bishop who once visited the island in 1895. It held the Catholic church, mission house, and the closed co-op sawmill. Twice a day the lay brother would ring the church bells, but few parishioners ever bothered to attend service – only the old and dying or those with nothing better to do. There was not one tree left standing on either island; they both appeared as though they had been sprayed with defoliant.

Throughout the village were dogs running wild and millions of black flies, mosquitoes, no-see-ums, and horse flies, all waiting for – almost expecting – the lonely man who descended from a floatplane not certain of what he might accomplish.

(2)

Brother André sat in the mission house kitchen slurping coffee out of a large mug. He dunked jam cookies into the mug, one after another, mashing down each cookie until it was paste before popping it into his mouth. Once he finished the package, he could feel his stomach bulge and his pants tighten. "*Je deviens gros,*" he thought. *I'm getting fat.* But then he put it out of his mind, crumpled the plastic, and placed the empty package in the waste basket. He quietly rose from his chair. Peeking at the crucifix hanging on the wall, he made the sign of the cross and lumbered outside to continue chopping wood. *Chop… Chop…Chop…Chop…*The sound echoed like a drum in an African jungle.

Above the kitchen, Father Benoît, a thin, older man with hairy arms, specks of white hair, and grey skin, lay in bed reciting the rosary. As he repeated the prayers, the rosary beads moved mechanically through his fingers. *"Pater Noster, qui es in caelis, sanctificetur nomen tuum… Ave maria, gratia plena, Dominus tecum..."*

When he finished, he could hear the chopping, over and over. *Chop…Chop…Chop…Chop… "Veux-tu donc arrêter!"* he whispered under his breath. *Won't you stop!* But the chopping continued. The younger cleric would not stop, could not stop, not until the last of twenty cords of wood were chopped, stacked, and stored in the empty sawmill. Later the wood would be distributed to the village elders, but the supply would never last long. Throughout the long, cold winter, the lay brother would travel by snow machine into the nearby forest to cut down trees. It was constant, hard work providing fuel wood for others – and it never seemed to end.

Father Benoît began to dress. He put on the same dark pants, plaid shirt, dark blue suspenders, and heavy leather boots that he did every day. The attire gave him the appearance of a French-Canadian farmer – *un habitant* – wearing a collar. When he stared into the silver-framed wall mirror, all he saw were sad, grey eyes. He peeked outside as Brother André lifted his axe with both hands, slammed down hard to split a piece of wood in half, and continued. *"Il va être faim,"* the priest thought. *He will be hungry.* He felt tired, drained, and much older than a man of seventy-eight, but he knew he would have to prepare lunch and supper for Brother André. More and more he was becoming the man's servant.

He walked down to the kitchen, which had the look and feel of a Gaspé farmhouse: all that was missing was the smells of freshly cut hay and ocean. He gathered butter, cheese, a freshly cooked ham, home-made bread, and Dijon mustard to make three ham and cheese sandwiches, one for himself and two for Brother André. Then he took down a kettle pot and began to make a stew. He did this slowly, carefully, pouring cold water into the pot, adding kidney beans, onions, potatoes, celery, pepper, salt, bay leaves, and finally frying up thick pieces of moose meat to add to the pot. Then Father Benoît took a pork roast, scored the meat, placed it into a pan, sprinkled salt and pepper, added butter, and placed the pan into the oven where it would cook slowly until the fat caramelized. He would serve the stew for supper and keep the pork for tomorrow.

When he sat down at the kitchen table, he could still hear the chopping outside. He wondered who would take on the duty of supplying the elders with fuel wood after he and Brother André left the village. There were fewer and fewer men entering the priesthood. He knew that when he left, no other priest would be sent as a replacement.

Father Benoît thought of the Mission House in Ottawa, where he would spend his final days praying with elderly priests in cassocks and walking beside the Rideau River, reciting rosaries. He lay his head on the table. He knew he was dying – "*Je meurs.*" He looked up at the crucifix and thought of God the Father, Son, and Holy Ghost; the angels and saints; and the Mother of God, the Virgin Mary. He imagined the peace and joy that would come with death and the vision of God. "*Le Seigneur m'attend,*" he thought. *The Lord is waiting for me.*

(3)

The abandoned cabin was at the furthest point on the mainland. After fifty years of wear and tear, there was hardly anything left but a shell of logs covered with a piece of worn-out canvas. Three villagers sat inside on the floor. The girl, Dorothy, was slender, smoking a cigarette. Except for pockmarks on her face, she was pretty. The band administrator, Luke, had a hard face, troubled eyes, and hair falling down over his shoulders. He wore a black tee shirt, black denim pants, and black leather boots. He drank homebrew out of a jar. The third villager, Henry, was drunk and lay spreadeagle on the floor. "U...steal...from...us," he said, looking at Luke. "U...write checks...fur...urself."

"Shut the fuck up," Luke said.

"U du...I sa u."

"I want you to go!"

"Doon...waanna...go!"

"I guess I have to teach you."

Luke reached over and slapped Henry in the face. "No more talking," he said.

"I goot a right to saay...waat...I want."

"No, you don't, not with me." Luke stood up and kicked Henry in the head, just above the eye socket. Henry rolled over and passed out.

"Please, Luke, don't hurt him anymore. He doesn't know what he's saying," the girl said.

"Don't tell me what I can or can't do, Dorothy. So, what if I steal from the band and write myself checks? The chief signs off on those checks. The old fool does what I tell him. I do what I want – you understand?!"

He continued to drink the grey, foul-smelling liquid. The girl bit her lip, worried he might explode, and continued to smoke as the ashes slowly started to fall.

The band administrator kept everything bottled up inside without uttering a word before suddenly yelling, screaming, or rattling off about people. He was complicated and difficult to understand. Dorothy was simple, young, and had no deep thoughts. In many ways, she thought and acted like a child.

"Give me a puff!" Luke said.

She lit a cigarette and passed it to him.

"Good girl," he said, and patted her on the head. She was about to say something but hesitated.

"Don't say anything, Dorothy, about us living together!" he warned. "Not now. I'll let you know when I'm ready."

She crouched like a beaten dog in a corner.

He dragged Henry outside and left him on one of the walkways. When he returned, he spoke soothingly. "Come here little one, come here. You know that I like you a lot." Dorothy stood, came up to him, and wrapped her arms around him.

"Are you, my girl?" he whispered softly.

"Yes," she replied.

"Good. But now I'm going outside for a walk. I need air. I need to think."

He walked outside and carried the jar of homebrew close to his chest. The lake was still and quiet. A raven flew by and touched his hair. He passed the abandoned Anglican church. When he reached the community dock he stood and looked across to the smaller island. He could easily see the Catholic church and mission house. "I could burn them down," he thought. Luke imagined the two buildings in flames, the tabernacle and confessional in ashes, the mission house a white, burning bonfire, and the two clerics running around in their underwear with buckets of water, trying to put out the fires. He laughed out loud. "I would like to see them running around like the two idiots they are. But they will be gone soon. Good riddance!" he thought. "Better we have no priests, brothers, or nuns. They lie and do no good. They feed on the people's weakness. God? There is no God, only liars."

Dorothy followed the walkway until she found Luke. She took his hand in hers and felt the warts on his fingers, the small, ugly clusters of grey skin that never went away. "You should see the nurse and get some medicine for the warts," she said.

"Some other time. Not now. I can always burn them off," he said. "Dorothy, I hate the village. There is nothing here – no future. Not for me, not for you, not for anyone. I hope everyone leaves and never comes back."

"But where will they go?" she asked.

The thought of the clerics running around half-naked trying to put out a fire crossed his mind. "Does it matter?" he said. "Someday the village will be moved and all of what you see will be gone. Nothing really matters – nothing. Those buildings you see could be burned to the ground; the whole village could be burned to the ground. Do you think it matters? Nothing matters – nothing."

"Don't say nothing." She squeezed his hand. "I love you."

He offered no reply, could barely think of anything to say. Then, reluctantly, he said, "I know."

(4)

The federal nursing station was out of place. It was a quaint house with a peaked roof, polite shutters, and a white picket fence, more suited to a town in the south than an isolated Indian village halfway to Hudson Bay. A visitor might easily expect to meet a sweet elderly couple instead of a Filipino nurse with a worried look.

The nurse who staffed the station had been hired on a temporary work permit with no guarantee that her one-year contract would be extended. Today, more so than ever, she felt it would not. She had good reason.

One of the village men had asked for Demerol; when she refused, he threatened her with a beating. She told him it was addictive, that his "bad headache" was simply a hangover, and she offered him Tylenol. He was not pleased. After being threatened by more than one villager for refusing to prescribe Demerol, she told the nurse supervisor at the Sioux Lookout Regional Zone Hospital that she was not going to be intimidated. "I told them they could threaten me all they wanted but I was not going to dispense narcotics unless there was a good reason!"

"Good for you, Nurse Gonzales," the nurse supervisor said.

"We can't have addicts running around in Windsor House; it's bad enough that they go on binges and cause all sorts of violence and mayhem."

But now she found herself searching for six bottles of Demerol that were missing from the locked medicine closet. She looked everywhere – the examination room, patient's room, living room, kitchen, even her own bedroom and the visitor's bedroom. "Where are you, Demerol?" she whispered. "Where did you disappear to?" But she found nothing.

Anna Gonzales was highly organized and not someone to make mistakes easily. She wore her hair short and dressed modestly. Everything about her spoke of a nurse dedicated to her profession. She imagined what the nurse supervisor would say when she discovered there were six missing bottles of Demerol. "How did you lose those bottles, Nurse Gonzales? Did you give them out to those men? Did you sell them to a 'friend'?" She might just as easily say "to a young handsome Indian man." Anna knew that the nurse supervisor had no love for a university-educated Filipino nurse with eight years of experience in a big Manila Hospital. The nurse supervisor would love nothing better than to terminate her contract and chase her back to the Philippines, back to her large, extended family who were hoping to emigrate to Canada.

"Why am I so stupid? Why do I let Nurse Chaffey bother me?" she thought. She had no easy answers. But she knew that her future, and that of her family, rested on finding the missing bottles. The Zone Hospital tracked everything in the nursing stations, especially controlled medicines and narcotics. "Sooner or later, they're going to find out that the bottles are missing. No matter what I say they won't believe me; I'll be forced to resign. After that no one will hire me. I'll have no choice but to go back to the Philippines." Her hopes for a better future rested on finding the bottles. But now it seemed that it was not to be.

Before Anna had arrived in the village, the nurse supervisor had told her, "I promise that you won't be in Windsor House very long. It is an awful place, not like any other village in the region. The local Indians charter planeloads of liquor and drink like there's no tomorrow. Women are raped, men beaten, and families torn apart. All of the nurses we ever send to Windsor House request a transfer. I expect you will, too. Of course, there's Father Benoît, a dear man, but unfortunately, he has a heart condition, I expect he will be leaving the village. You have only yourself, only your strength and discipline to handle your responsibilities. As long as you stay professional, keep all the medicines locked and secure, treat patients, and don't get too friendly, you should be fine. When your contract ends, I think I can promise a better posting."

The nurse supervisor had also warned her not to travel to outpost camps. "Remember, you're not a missionary, you're a resident nurse. The Indians come to you – not you to them. It's safer that way. God knows they might take advantage of you way out there all alone, a single woman. No, no, you can't travel to any of the outpost camps."

Since arriving in Windsor House, the nurse had travelled to two outpost camps with an Indian guide in a freighter canoe. On her first trip she treated an elderly man dying of stomach cancer and on her second trip, a woman giving birth. Both trips were safe, even enjoyable, with moments of discovery. She ate traditional food, heard family laughter, went swimming, and sat by a fire listening to an elderly woman tell her about the world and universe. Anna learned more about Ojibwa culture and traditions and herself than she would have if she stayed locked up in the nursing station. She learned she was like these people! And her perspective on them became more favourable. She never told any of this to the nurse supervisor. "I go where I'm needed," she thought. "Why else did I become a nurse?"

Nurse Gonzales continued to search throughout the nursing station for the missing bottles. She found nothing. In the early evening she sat down and wondered who might have stolen them. If it was the men who asked for painkillers, they could have easily broken into the nursing station and stolen the Demerol, especially when she was traveling to the outpost camps. But no doors or windows were broken and the medicine closet showed no signs of being broken into. It could have been a visiting patient – perhaps the door to the medicine closet had been left open when she was busy? It could have been the woman who cleaned the station, perhaps using a tool to open the closet? It could have been anyone. "I could tell Nurse Chaffey that some of the local women stopped by for tea and one of them stole the Demerol, but who, which woman, and why would I have left the closet door open?" She imagined different women sipping tea and one of them slipping away and stealing the Demerol. A number of family surnames popped into her head – Atlookan, Waboose, Anderson, and Slipperjack. But she could never settle on a face to place the blame.

She undressed and stared at herself in the bathroom mirror: a short, unattractive prisoner with flat breasts, waiting to be shot. She started a bath, played a record, and lay in the soapy hot water. The singer's voice rose slowly from the record player:

> The way you hold your knife
> The way we danced 'til three
> The way you changed my life
> No, no, they can't take that away from me
> No, they can't take that away from me

"What will they do?" Anna thought.

(5)

The house was tidy, clean, and well organized, with a front porch to store hunting and fishing equipment – traps, fishnets, waders, twine, steel tubs, axes, and guns. An older Ojibwa woman with long hair and a flowered dress swept the kitchen floor. Her daughter watched as she rocked her own newborn son. "We should be on the river," her mother said, "We should be at camp. We should not take chances, staying here for long; any day now someone is going to charter a load of whiskey. I can feel it in my bones, April. I don't want us to be here. You understand, don't you? I don't think I'm being foolish."

"No, Mother, you're not being foolish."

"I only worry about you, the baby, and your father."

"I know."

Her mother worried about the drinking and violence; it often seemed like a terrible epidemic had arrived and settled in Windsor House, one that would not leave. Her mother complained about her father like she always did when things were not as they should be. "He never listens to me, not really. Even when we were first married, even then he was stubborn. 'I know what we will do,' he would tell me, and I would listen and follow him. In 1957, you were a young girl when we settled in Windsor House. It was quiet and safe then, and we all went to church regularly to hear Father Benoît. It was where you and your brothers were baptized, confirmed, and received communion. But everything has changed and Father Benoît is leaving. We all know he will not be returning."

She watched her mother sweeping even the smallest bits of dirt away. She listened, knowing no good would come from an argument. She continued to rock the baby in a cradle board – a *tiganakan* – that had held many other babies.

"What do you think?' her mother asked.

"Yes, Mother, I agree that we should leave. But can't we stay for a few more days? Everything seems quiet now. When I walk around all I hear is quiet."

"Listen to me, listen to your old mother…" and she listed all the reasons why they should return to their camp and why staying in Windsor House was dangerous: people made homebrew; they stole; they beat each other; eight months earlier a man had beaten his wife and taken her to an outpost camp, and she was never seen or heard from again; children were hiding in vacant houses and sniffing gas; there was no resident police officer to protect people; and it was only a matter of time before someone arranged for a charter of liquor and the serious drinking began. There was nothing safe about the village, nothing at all.

"Mother, I don't think that many people are drinking now. I don't think we need to run away. Besides, this is where we live, and we only returned two days ago. I don't think two more days will make a difference."

"It does matter," her mother replied. "Every day matters. Nothing is good any more. No other village suffers like Windsor House. The school is closed – how could Indian Affairs do that, keep the school closed for a year? – and no one cares. Why should we stay?"

The woman's father was a tall man with jet-black hair. He was carving an eagle's head out back, near the shed. It was a warm day with a light breeze. All the bits and pieces of cedar fell onto the earth in a pile, leaving the clean smell of cedar in the air. His hands were strong and weathered – yet they worked with the wood in a soft and gentle way, as though he were slowly falling in love with the wood. He worked on the eyes, beak, neck, talons, and feathers so that they were rich in detail. He was careful with his tools. His chisels, gougers, veiners, and bench knives were repeatedly filed and oiled and well taken care of. At one point he thought, "I could paint an eagle high on a tree looking down over a nest. I would paint the eyes yellow, head white, feathers brown, and talons black."

He often stopped to fill his pipe with tobacco. When he did, he looked at the clouds and listened to the ravens. "Oh, Raven, you talk so much, you have no time to see."

His daughter came out. "Father, do you think we can go tomorrow?" she asked.

"Is she pestering you?" he asked.

"Yes."

His wife was always impatient to leave when they had just returned. He knew she preferred the camp, where it was safe and quiet. But he enjoyed the village knowing what it had been and what he believed it might be once again, a warm and friendly place. He had no fear of the drinkers. "Tell her we will return in three days," he said.

"She won't be happy."

"I know – but tell her that in three days we can leave and return to camp." His daughter heard the baby cry and returned to the kitchen.

"Is he hungry?" her mother asked.

"No – I just fed him. He wants attention and needs to be rocked."

The baby had the face of her late husband. Whenever she held the baby, she saw the dimples and mischievous smile. When she began to rock, the baby stopped crying and went to sleep.

April had a college diploma as a practical nurse. She had worked in the Thunder Bay Port Arthur General Hospital for two years and knew the city well. Her two boys waited at the outpost camp with her brother and sister-in-law and their three children. Her late husband had been a band carpenter and would tease her about going to university to become a registered nurse. "You could work as the resident nurse and I could build houses," he would say.

"I love you so very much," she thought, as though he were still alive.

She imagined their return trip, travelling by freighter canoe. They would stop at Second Rapids; from the shoreline she would watch her father steer the freighter canoe through the rapids, using the motor to tack back and forth. She would gather blueberries, pin cherries, and gooseberries, peppermint, burdock, bearberry, and red willow leaves. They would travel along the river until they came to the lake, where she would see the loons fishing and her boys calling out.

She wondered if Indian Affairs would reopen the school. If it stayed closed, she would move to Thunder Bay. "I want my boys to be educated so they can work," she thought. "Whether in a city or village, it doesn't matter."

She returned to the kitchen, made tea, took dry meat out of the fridge, and brought them out to her father. Her husband had died in the winter driving a tractor train, pulling a heavy load of fuel, when it fell through the ice. When she looked at the baby, she thought of her dead husband as though he were still alive – as though she, too, had hope, as though there was hope for the village.

"Did you say something?" her mother asked.

"No, I was only thinking of *him*."

(6)

It was dark in the warehouse except for the light from a dim yellow bulb on the ceiling. Among the stacked cases of food, dry goods, and clothing was the shadow of a heavy-set man wearing a hearing aid. Now and then, the Hudson's Bay relief store manager called out, "Hello?" His high voice sounded like a counter tenor in a sad opera.

The manager was waiting for a local middle-aged woman he had hired to help him do inventory. The woman had shown up in the store desperate for work. "I have very little work in the store and I already have a part-time clerk," he told her. But then he hired her anyway. "You can help me with inventory," he said. They agreed to meet in the afternoon at the warehouse.

When the woman knocked on the door, he failed to hear her. She wondered why she had come to the warehouse knowing that the relief manager would likely want to have sex. Why else would anyone hire a woman who was passed around from one man to another like a worn-out mocassin? But she had no one else to turn to and needed the money to buy food and cigarettes. She was a lost soul.

She walked to the store, peeked inside, saw that everything was quiet, and decided to check the manager's house. When she peeked through the open curtains, all she saw were dishes stacked on top of a coffee table, ashtrays full of cigarette butts, and magazines scattered all over the floor. She returned to the warehouse and sat on the steps.

When the relief manager found her, he led her back to the warehouse and began to undress her. When he finished, she asked. "Do you want me to stay?"

"No," he replied. "Maybe tomorrow we can do inventory, but I'll let you know. I'll open the store tonight so you can come over and buy what you want. If you want, you can stay and come to my house later and we can… well, we can do something."

After she left, he sat down and thought of Winnipeg in the summer when the Red River flowed through the city – the thick bushes, the sweltering heat, and the downtown apartment where he lived alone, divorced, and often drunk. "I might tell her to visit me if she comes to Winnipeg." But then he had second thoughts. "It might be better if I leave her alone."

Chapter 2

DISCOVERY

(1)

The shoreline was littered with garbage, bottles, gasoline cans, discarded diapers, every imaginable type of household waste – even a dog's carcass lay on the shore, its eyes filled with maggots. The dried, shriveled body picked over by ravens served as a warning sign: Do Not Enter!

When Rager stepped out of the plane and onto the community dock, it seemed like a signal; the blackflies descended. "They're just saying hello," the pilot said in a welcoming tone.

"Good for the blackflies, but I don't need their hello," Rager replied, swatting and doing his best to chase them away.

"I don't think I've ever seen this many blackflies this late in the season," the pilot commented. "It's usually only in June when they get this bad. Must be because of the garbage. See, no one bothers to collect and burn the garbage, not a damn thing, and that's a problem. They used to, but now, maybe once in a while. Generally, the villagers let everything rot – it really is something!" He pointed to the dog carcass. "But it could be worse," he said. "It could be a human corpse."

Rager stood in awe, uncertain of what to say.

"There really is no place like Windsor House," the pilot said, "At least in this region, for garbage, blackflies, drinking, and violence, I would say it's unique." The dock was empty and the silence deafening.

Rager thought out loud. "I wonder where everyone is."

"Probably waiting for you."

"I hope so."

"Good luck on that."

The pilot climbed back into the cockpit. It was a signal for them to part. Rager picked up his bags and began to walk along one of the walkways. He came to the agency cabin; the front window was broken and covered with a sheet of plywood. When he walked inside, he discovered dried vomit on the sofa, broken beds in the bedrooms, dirty dishes piled high in the sink, and rotten food in the fridge. He spent the next hour cleaning and making a bed. Then he left in search of the band administrator, hoping he could arrange a meeting with the chief and council that very evening, if possible. He had no desire to stay in the village very long. As was his custom, he carried a notebook and pen.

He walked until he found Luke sitting in a wheelbarrow, smoking a cigarette. Somewhat surprised to see a man he had met only once, Luke asked "What brings you here?" Rager was equally surprised to see the band administrator sitting comfortably in a wheelbarrow with apparently not a care in the world. It suddenly struck him as being very silly: two men meeting, one sitting in a wheelbarrow, the other standing holding a notepad, walkways zig-zagging every which way, and insects whirling about.

"Luke, I came because Mr. Reed asked me to. Sister Brunelle wrote a letter to the regional director general complaining that the district office doesn't do enough to support Windsor House. Mr. Reed asked me to consult with your chief and council on steps we can take to support the village. Do you think I could meet with the chief and council, tonight if possible?"

Luke had no respect for government officials generally, and even less so for Indian Affairs officials, but the man standing in front of him seemed to be different. He thought for a moment before answering. "I don't know if we have enough councilors to make up a quorum, John. I'll have to look around."

"Can you find out and let me know?"

"Sure, I can do that." Luke wondered where the conversation might lead.

"Do you remember when I was last here, we talked briefly about the five-district fly-in villages starting a development corporation and taking over ownership of the agency sport-fishing camps? At the time, you told me it was a great idea."

"I remember; I don't easily forget. Has anything happened?"

"Not yet. I need regional approval to initiate the planning process. Anyway, we can talk about that and anything else the chief and council want to discuss."

"You know that the province is talking about building airstrips next to the villages?"

"No, I didn't."

"Well, they are. Tells you a lot about your own agency that you don't know. I guess that Reed never tells his own staff what's happening. But if that goes ahead, Windsor House will have to be relocated to a site with more land so we can build an airstrip. Two islands won't cut it – you'd have to build an airstrip over the water. I don't think that's in the cards."

Somewhat embarrassed at not knowing about all this, Rager replied, "It's the first I've heard of the airstrips, but that would be good news. It would mean no more three-week periods of freeze-up and break-up when float planes can't get into the village."

"It means a lot more than that," Luke replied. "During freeze-up and break-up, if anyone gets very sick the zone hospital has to send in a helicopter. If the weather is poor there is no helicopter, and someone can die. We also don't have any fresh food deliveries. If we had an airstrip, we could use wheeled aircraft year-round; it would lower transportation costs on food, fuel, travel, just about everything." A Cheshire smile crept over his face.

"Where would you build the new village?" Rager asked.

"Not far from here, about two kilometers, and not on any islands!"

"Why did they build the village on the islands in the first place?"

"I guess the government never thought we deserved an airstrip, just like we never deserved water and sewage."

"Poor planning?"

"How about saving money? The government doesn't spend money on people who have no political power. Do you think anyone gives a damn about any Indian village in Canada, let alone up here in our region? Hell, the average Canadian hardly knows where we live, let alone who we are. I guess they think we grew out of the ground?"

Bristol flashed across Rager's mind: it was a permanent cicatrice, and now there was Windsor House. "Why am I here?" he wondered.

"Negotiations between the federal and provincial government are never easy," Rager said. "So, the chief and council need to think of what the agency can do in the short term. Do you have any suggestions?"

"Reopen the school and the sawmill. Of course, the school will have to be repaired and the sawmill subsidized, but it would signal to everyone that the government is serious about making improvements. Those with kids will have a good reason to stay in the village, and with the sawmill, not only do you create seasonal jobs, but you save on the transportation cost of imported lumber. That's another thing – we need lumber to repair the houses, too. Many have mold and need to be renovated. If Indian Affairs supported a development corporation and transferred ownership of the camps to the corporation, that would also signal that you're serious about economic development." Then Luke added, "Everyone needs hope, John."

"Any other ideas?"

Luke widened his smile; he had a strange mischievous look. "How about a coffee shop where people can socialize, you know, sit around and gossip? Much better than a wheelbarrow. Maybe it's something that I could own? What do you think, John, don't I look like an entrepreneur?"

"Why is this man mocking me?" Rager thought. "What did I ever do to him? Am I a proxy for government fools?"

"Don't you already have a job, Luke?" he asked.

"I could do it as a side business."

"If the chief and council agree, I suppose so."

"They will – believe me, they will." Luke smiled knowingly.

Rager decided to give the band administrator a bit of his own medicine. "The Manpower Local Initiative Project, what did the band do with the funding, Luke? We keep getting copies of letters addressed to you, requesting a report on what was accomplished. Do you know anything about that?"

Luke took his time before answering. "You mean the contribution funds?"

"Yes, how was the money spent?"

"A few houses were painted…and others repaired…why?"

"Manpower expects a report. Otherwise, Manpower will demand that the band return all funds. By the way, I'm only trying to help you. I'm not the inquisitor. Do you have before and after pictures of the houses?

"To answer your question, no."

"Any records of what was purchased and who was employed?"

"Sorry, but the band records were stolen."

"So, no records, absolutely nothing, am I right?"

"Nothing – zero – the records are all gone."

Luke knew that nothing would be done. He stepped out of the wheelbarrow.

"Time to go, John, time to go. Come over to the band office at eight o'clock. I'll do what I can to round up as many councilors as possible. With the school closed there aren't many people in the village, so I can't promise a full council. By the way, closing the school and keeping it closed for over a year was a decision taken by your agency, the Department of Indian Affairs and Northern Development Nakina District, with no consultation. A bit ironic, don't you think, that they send you up here asking us how they can, oh, let me quote your own words, 'support the village'?"

Luke walked away, leaving the commerce officer standing alone, wondering what to expect.

At eight o'clock, Rager walked to the band office. There were four people waiting: Luke, the elderly and unilingual chief, and two councilors. Luke started the meeting and served as translator to the chief.

After an hour of discussion, they agreed that, in the long term, the village would have to be relocated for an airstrip, but in the short term, there were five priorities: reopen the school; lobby the province to place a resident police officer with a holding cell in the village; open and subsidize the co-op sawmill; repair a dozen houses suffering with mold; and establish a five-fly-in-village development corporation to own and operate the camps. Luke commented, "Indian Affairs should never have owned the sportfishing camps. The agency can't even figure out how to keep a school open. Why would they do any better with operating the camps?" He added, as a final point, "I can tell you this: if nothing happens, if Indian Affairs doesn't follow up on those priorities, I guarantee you that soon there won't be anyone left in Windsor House." He stared directly at Rager and asked seriously, "Would you stay, John?"

"No – I would go. I'm amazed that anyone stays now, what with the school closed."

Luke and the chief spoke together.

"What are you talking about?" Rager asked.

"He say's, John, not to think of just the village as our home. Look at all the land and water around here. That's where we come from. Even though the government wants us gone, it's not going to happen. We have traditional camps; we use those camps to hunt, trap, and fish. We have burial sites. We have sacred sites. We go back a long way. The land is us, John. The government has no right to tell us anything. The village is just a place that can be moved. Do you understand?" His voice was gruff. He offered no mischievous smile. He was deadly serious.

Rager nodded agreement. When he left the meeting, he knew that Luke was more than a band administrator – he spoke like a chief.

(2)

Rager knew that Father Benoît would know a great deal. So, the following morning, he walked over to see the priest. After explaining the reason for his trip, the two men sat together in the mission living room. It had the look and feel of another time: a hand-made bookcase and table, wooden chairs, the picture of Pope John XXIII hanging on the wall next to a crucifix, and a radio transmitter with tubes and wires.

Rager began by letting the priest know what the chief and council had agreed upon as priorities to revitalize the village. The priest said, "I agree with everything. The school should never have been closed; it should have been repaired. It was a decision that your supervisor of education took with Mr. Reed's support and, I might add, with no consultation – even after I told them both that the consequences would be terrible for the villagers.

"We need a police presence to curb the violence and drinking, but that has not happened because of funding disagreements between the two levels of government. I lobbied Mr. Reed to continue these efforts, but nothing has ever been done.

"The co-op sawmill equipment needs to be inspected, but I believe the sawmill can be reopened at minimal cost. The government will have to subsidize the operation, but there would be considerable savings if we could use a local resource to repair houses instead of importing lumber. It would serve as a form of 'import substitution.'

"I agree that a number of houses need to be repaired because of the problem of mold; too many of our houses were built cheaply by outside contractors.

"I agree that a development corporation is a sound proposition, especially since you are talking about setting up a corporation with five different bands; it would concentrate ownership and capital into one corporate entity. With good management and, new investment, I have no reason to doubt that it would be successful.

"In summary, the five priorities are a good beginning to revitalize Windsor House. As for relocating the village, I can tell you that the village should never have been built on two islands with so little room for expansion, let alone constructing an airstrip. So yes, eventually the village will have to be relocated. It would have made more sense to have the church, mission house, and Hudson's Bay store rebuilt on a site with adequate land for a village *and* future expansion, and not the other way around." Then he added, sadly, "The government never plans anything properly. They always operate on their own, often creating more problems than they solve."

After he spoke, he looked pale. He placed his hand over his heart and seemed to be in pain. "Excuse me," he said. He retreated to the kitchen, where he took a nitro-glycerine tablet before returning.

"Father Benoît, how long have you been in the region?" Rager asked.

"I arrived in 1927, so almost fifty years."

"Is there anything I should know about the past, anything that would help me understand how we came to where we are today? If you could tell me, it would help me a great deal. If nothing else, as a government we should avoid past failures."

The priest began by describing a world that no longer existed. In a radius of sixty kilometers there were traditional camps, comprised of extended family groupings, where the men hunted and trapped in small units and the women took care of the children. Up to the late 1950s, the people lived in these camps, independent of government except for the law that forced them to send their children to residential school. As for government support, they received very little funding – except for the small, four-dollar annuity for every man, woman, and child guaranteed by the 1905 treaty. In 1927, those aged seventy years and older began to receive an old age benefit of $240 per year; and starting in 1946, parents of school-age children received a monthly family allowance of eight dollars per child; altogether, very little money.

But the residential school system changed everything. Over time, parents and grandparents could see the changes in their children. Too often, children returned as strangers, unable to properly speak their own language, unable to know their own culture, unable to forgive the feeling of abandonment. In response to complaints from parents and grandparents, the government decided to build in villages primary schools to keep families together, with the expectation that, when they were older, they would be sent to residential schools. But there were other problems.

The creation of villages led to a decline in trapping; instead of people living in scattered camps spread out over vast, abundant, fur-bearing areas, they were concentrated into small villages where there were few opportunities to make a living. In response, the government brought in make-work and training programs. But for the most part, these programs were a failure. With the make-work programs, too often more people were hired than were needed; in many cases only to stand around and feel foolish. The training programs led nowhere because there were few employment opportunities in the villages. In less than a decade, government policy had turned an independent, nomadic, self-reliant people into a welfare ghetto.

He concluded. "I am an old man now not long for this world. I am no longer certain of as many beliefs as I once held as a young priest. My mind wanders often to the deep silence on the trail, the dog team pulling me as I steer a sled, with the sun on my face and the wind at my back. It is a disgrace the way the government has operated, the way they treated Indians. If these people were white, it would never have happened, but with Indians it was another matter.

"You know Mr. Reed never visits our village. It is always myself, or the chief, or Luke who travel to Grayson to see him. It is never the other way around. When I do see him, I always feel like a beggar with his hand stretched out. If I were a blind man with a tin cup and a cane, it would make no difference. All I see is an older man sitting at a desk who does nothing, feels nothing, and thinks only of his own welfare."

Father Benoît felt the pain in his chest again and stopped speaking. He wondered inwardly, "All this talking, this lecturing, to a new government official, someone who appears sincere, but what can possibly change?"

"Father, I hope my visit leads to better living conditions," Rager said. "I certainly hope that my report isn't shelved. I also plan to travel to Toronto regional office to lobby the regional director general. I'm told that David Stewart is not a career civil servant, but a university professor on a leave of absence hired to implement new and innovative ways of delivering programs and services.

I'm certain he'll support what the chief and council are requesting. Mr. Reed is a minor official. He doesn't control everything. Thankfully, he retires in the New Year. After that, I certainly hope there is improvement."

"I hope so too, Monsieur. I hope this plan helps the village. I have never seen it so bad; never in my life have I witnessed such drinking, violence, and despair! The village is dying."

The living room was worn down. A deep, unsettling gloom came over both men. Rager imagined the many different meetings that had taken place between the priest and government officials, nurses, teachers, Ontario Hydro officials, mining exploration company officials, police seeking advice after making an arrest, a long line of people who had come to the village for one reason or another while others who sat in the chair would have been the villagers themselves: elders, chiefs, councilors, husbands and wives, mothers and fathers, and children. Over the course of fifty years, over a thousand people had spoken with this one priest, their faces appearing, speaking, and watching him year after year as he grew older. The room had witnessed the creation of a village and now was witnessing its likely demise. The priest, too, was worn down, like an old snow machine that has a bad engine; no amount of repair can save it from being towed out to the dump and discarded.

Their discussion was coming to an end when Rager decided to raise a subject that intrigued him. "Father, can you tell me about the event that happened four years ago that led to the Anglicans leaving the village?"

"It was an unpredictable event," Father Benoît replied. "It was something that I never saw before and I will never forget. I have my own thoughts on why it happened, but you can draw your own conclusions."

(3)

"What do we know about people?" the priest began. "What do we really know? In many ways, each of us is a mystery and we can only guess what each of us is thinking. We talk and we listen to each other, we try to connect, and more often than not, we fail. But there are times when one man can affect what others think and come to believe. They almost have a power to control people. They do it through what – their own beliefs, their own will, or is it through something deeper, through reaching out to what the people themselves want to believe?

"A prophet is like that: he works with a willing audience, much like a magician who plays tricks works with those who want to believe. Perhaps it is best to say that after all the changes in their lives, the Anglicans who had moved into Windsor House were ready for what was to happen. They wanted to believe; they wanted the world to end.

"It started in October, 1972. Noah Anderson was his name – he was *the prophet*, a thirty-eight-year-old trapper, a bachelor, an Anglican; a man with no brothers or sisters, a man who lived in the village, but more often lived with his elderly parents in an outpost camp. He was someone who kept to himself; someone you might see now and then in the village trading furs or buying supplies. He was a man who did everything alone – trapping, hunting, and fishing – and was never known to have been with a woman, at least not that I know of. From what I was told, he attended church on a regular basis, or as much as he could, but he was never someone considered overly religious. I suppose that is why when it happened, when he experienced his vision, it shattered what the people had come to believe about Noah. It made them think that what he experienced, perhaps, was true.

"This is what he told everyone:

"'I was alone, hunting on the Attawapiskat River. I turned off onto the Martin Falls Drinking River. At one point, the river changed direction and began to flow towards a great light. I found that I no longer had control over the boat. Suddenly it was the river that had control, and it pulled me towards the light.

"'After some time, I heard a voice calling me, "Noah, come to me, my son…Draw closer, do not be afraid, my son…Come to me…Come." Soon, I saw a man standing on a hill with a great multitude of people sitting at the base of the hill listening to him. The man was clothed in a long white robe with a golden girdle around his breast. His hair was long and dark, his eyes radiant. On his feet were bronze sandals and there was a halo around his head. In his right hand he held seven stars. The man looked at me and saw that I was terrified. He repeated the same words, "Noah, come to me my son. Do not be afraid. I am Jesus Christ, the only son of God, the savior who was sent to save the world." And so, I let the river pull me towards him until I reached shore, where the people parted and let me sit.

"'Jesus spoke to the multitude. He said the world would soon enter a period of tribulation when seven angels would descend from Heaven onto Earth. Each angel would carry a bowl of wrath. The first bowl would unleash foul-smelling sores onto men; the second would destroy the seas and oceans; the third would turn rivers and lakes into blood; the fourth would turn the sun into a ball of fire; the fifth would unleash Hell – a deep, fathomless pit full of dragons, serpents, and demons where Satan sat on a throne in the middle of a burning lake; the sixth would unleash Armageddon, when good and evil, angels and demons, would enter into a great battle; and the seventh would unleash an earthquake that would destroy all the cities and nations.

"'Jesus said that after Armageddon he would descend triumphantly from Heaven, leading a great host of angels to judge both the living and dead. Those who were saved would live for eternity in a new Jerusalem – a city of gold filled with jewels, where there would be no desire or sin, no beginning or end, no time, only spirit – with God the Father, the Alpha and Omega, the beginning and end, sitting in his golden throne triumphant. Those who were dammed would spend eternity in hell with Satan. Jesus said that the period of tribulation would begin on Easter Sunday, April 2, 1972.'

"Noah returned to his freighter canoe, no doubt traumatized by what he had witnessed, and immediately travelled to his parents' camp to tell them everything. At first, they were skeptical – no doubt they thought their son was sick, delusional, and perhaps they hoped that it would pass.

But it never did pass. If anything, his behavior became much worse. Noah stopped sleeping and eating; instead, day and night he pored through the bible, attempting to find comfort in what was written, and to Noah every word was a testament to God's power and will. When Peter denied knowing Jesus, it was to show the weakness in even the strongest of believers. When Jesus said on the cross, 'Father…Father…forgive them, for they know not what they do,' it was a statement that God would forgive even the foulest of men as long as they sought forgiveness. The Book of Revelation held a particular fascination because much of what Noah described is written there – in particular, the seven angels with their bowls of wrath, and Satan sitting on a throne in the middle of a burning lake of fire. The biblical descriptions confirmed that what Noah had heard was, in fact, the true word of God.

"When Noah's parents saw the changes in their son and that he was not going to go back to the way he had been before, they became frightened. You must remember that all his adult life, Noah had always been a quiet man, not given to speaking out. But now, suddenly, he was transformed into a great prophet who had witnessed Jesus predicting the end of the world on Easter Sunday.

"There were also the physical changes: Noah's eyes were full of rapture, he couldn't stand still, he quoted verses non-stop from the bible, at times shouting as though possessed by a great spirit before collapsing, exhausted, into a deep trance where he alone could hear Jesus' speaking. As much as his unshakable belief in the prophesy, these physical changes deeply affected his parents. They agreed he should travel to Windsor House and share his vision with the Anglican congregation.

"At the time, Windsor House had no resident Anglican minister and the congregation relied on local leaders. Reverend Lockwood lived in Sioux Lookout and would visit the village twice a year. This was not the case with the Catholics, for whom I was the resident priest. There was no one in authority within the Anglican congregation to challenge Noah's beliefs – no one to say, 'Noah, you have no proof, no witness to what you are telling us. How do we know that it is not your imagination playing a trick? A man travelling alone on a river can easily delude himself.'

"Instead, Noah was free to tell his story to a receptive audience. History is full of such events where people who have experienced a crisis – perhaps a plague, famine, war, or an event or series of events where they lose all control over their lives – turn to a supernatural explanation. It is not the first time this has happened and it will not be the last. 'Beware of false prophets' is not without precedence, especially when the false prophet believes in what he or she is saying. If you research the literature, you will read stories of 'crisis cults' and 'false prophets' going back millennia. I believe it was the same with Noah. The Anglicans had experienced great changes in their lives and no longer lived a traditional life, but were reliant on government. In a way they had experienced the end of the world, and they turned to a supernatural explanation. Noah's vision gave them that explanation.

"When Noah appeared in the village, he focused on converting two families. He told them what he had witnessed: he described the hill beside the river with a great multitude of people listening to a man in a white robe with a golden girdle around his breast, a halo around his head, and holding seven stars. He described what Jesus foretold and selected the most descriptive and frightening words: Hell as a bottomless pit full of demons and serpents and a lake of fire with Satan sitting on a throne; Armageddon as a great battle between the forces of good and evil, angels and demons; and finally, Jesus triumphant, descending from Heaven, leading a host of angels to judge both the living and dead. The physical change in Noah lent weight to his words. Here was a quiet man who had miraculously turned into a great orator. It forced people to think that perhaps what he was saying was true.

"Noah adopted two disciples: the Anglican deacon, who was a well-respected family man, and a man who served as community organizer. Together they legitimized what Noah was saying. In less than a month, the Anglican congregation – well over two hundred and fifty people, half the village – were believers. Once this happened, they pulled their children from school and began to meet daily in church, preparing for what they saw as a Day of Judgement.

"In early January, Reverend Lockwood arrived in the village. At first, he could not believe what had happened and he came to me for advice. 'What should I do?' he asked.

I told him to be patient. 'Give it time and the problem will resolve itself. On Easter Sunday the world will not end and the members of your congregation will come to their senses.' He agreed and left the village. I expect he was greatly saddened; after all, this was his congregation.

"Over the following weeks, the Anglican congregation turned inward. They attended church daily and women took turns to cook meals and care for the children. Whenever you passed the Anglican church, you could hear people praying, crying, and asking for God's forgiveness. It was constant, with Noah encouraging people to tell of their sins and ask forgiveness.

"By then the village was divided into two camps. On one side were all the Anglicans who were true believers; on the opposite were the Catholics who were nonbelievers. As the resident Catholic priest, I felt that I understood my congregation. Nonetheless, over time I saw the effect of the prophesy on my congregation. You must remember that the villagers spoke the same language, shared traditional customs and beliefs, and many were related through marriage. It was not unusual for an Anglican and Catholic to go out hunting or fishing together or to have their children play together. They were a community, albeit a community divided on religious lines, but still very much a community.

"The changes within the Catholic congregation were gradual. Someone might ask me if I thought Noah was speaking the truth. I said no, I didn't believe the end of the world would arrive on Easter Sunday. But over time I could see the increasing doubt in people's eyes. Imagine if half of your own community began to believe in a terrible event, perhaps a scientist predicting that an asteroid would strike the earth, would you not be tempted to believe?

"By mid-February the Anglican church was full of people praying and chanting daily. At that point, Noah and his two disciples decided to charter a plane and visit four nearby villages to warn people of the impending end of the world. Their visits were futile, however, because Reverend Lockwood had prepared the villages to beware of Noah.

They followed this with a trip to Timmins to meet the Anglican bishop. I suppose they felt that he would listen to what they had to say. But here, too, they failed; the bishop was furious and told them to stop.

What should have caused them to re-think their belief in the prediction only encouraged them to hold onto their belief. When they returned to Windsor House, they were convinced of their cause more than ever, and so were the Anglicans in the village. The refusal of others, if anything, only strengthened them in their belief. I think by then they had invested too much of themselves in the prophesy.

"As Easter Sunday approached, men and women stopped sleeping, many stopped eating, and some even began to speak in tongues – it was as though they were possessed by a supernatural force. All of this had a great effect on my own congregation. People kept asking me, 'Father, I am frightened, I cannot sleep at night, I have dreams of the end of the world. What if what they say is true?' I could see that they were beginning to have doubts. I started to fear that I might lose my congregation. I could not, and would not, let this happen. As a result, I decided to carefully set a trap.

"I summoned Noah and asked for a community meeting with both the Anglicans and Catholics. I said that it would provide him the opportunity to present his arguments to everyone. I knew it was an opportunity he could not pass up.

"We held the meeting with well over four hundred people in the community hall. Noah and his two disciples stood on the stage. Each quoted from the bible and Noah spoke last. When he finished, I rose quietly and walked up to the stage with a copy of the King James version of the bible, the same bible the Anglicans use and the one from which they took all their quotations.

"I held the bible up so everyone could see it. I pointed to it. I let my voice rise, 'The bible I hold is your very own bible,' I said. 'It is the King James Version of the Bible. It holds the true spoken words of God. But we must observe everything that is written in the bible. We cannot leave anything out. So, let us look at what the bible says about the end of the world.' I quoted Matthew 24:36, where Jesus says, 'But of that day and hour no one knows, not even the angels of heaven, nor the Son but the Father only.' When I finished, I looked at Noah. 'Explain to me Noah, how can this be? You tell us that God has given you the precise date for the end of the world, but in the bible, the true written word of God, Jesus says that no man, not even the angels in heaven, not even Jesus himself, will know the date.'

"I let my words sink in so everyone could think. Then I asked, 'If Jesus himself, the son of God, says no one can know the date, how can you know? I can only conclude that either God is crazy or you are crazy. We cannot have both.' I added, because it needed to be said, 'And I don't think that God, the creator of the universe and all life on Earth, is crazy! I have no more to say.' I walked to the back of the church and sat down.

"As soon as I did, the Catholics began to laugh. When I left, they followed me.

"Easter Sunday turned out to be a beautiful day. As the day progressed, there was no appearance of angels descending from heaven, and the Anglicans who had gathered in church began to leave, one by one. At the end of the day there was no one left in the Anglican church. The following week, Noah and his two disciples left the village. They returned much later, each man arriving in the village one at a time, with Noah the last to arrive.

"What followed was tragic. The Catholics began to ridicule the Anglicans – to say how stupid and gullible they had been to listen to Noah. I pleaded with them not to, but they continued. In a matter of weeks, the Anglican leadership decided to establish a new village forty kilometers to the north on a traditional site. One by one, they left and began to build what is now the village of Big Beaver House.

"As the Anglicans built the village, they asked Mr. Reed for government support for houses, a school, a nursing station, and programs and services. He refused outright. They petitioned the regional office and, after a number of meetings where they made it clear that they would never return to Windsor House, they received approval.

Within two years of their departure, Big Beaver House had houses, a school, a nursing station, and a full range of government programs and services.

"However, in Windsor House it was the exact opposite. The village was left with empty houses and buildings, a half-empty school, and a cut in programs and services – more than was warranted by the decline in population. The cuts were so severe to the point that the villagers wondered why they were being punished. When Indian Affairs closed the school a year ago and pulled out the teachers, it only added to the sense of abandonment. Today, what you see is a village on the verge of collapse. I appealed to Mr. Reed and many others, but my appeals went nowhere.

"With all of these events, you have to wonder what lies ahead. To me, the villagers – whether Catholic or Anglican – are pawns in the hands of government. The government rewards some and punishes others. They do so to show that they will not tolerate a divided village. Mr. Reed also does not like Windsor House or our band administrator."

"Why?"

"Because Luke detests Indian Affairs."

"Is it the budget cuts?"

"You must ask Luke. There are things a priest cannot say. A priest takes many things to the grave. It is, in many ways, a curse. You know that secrets kill people, and that is why the church offers the sacrament of confession. Governments have secrets, too, you know. Everyone, including Mr. Reed, has secrets. Even you, I would think, Monsieur, have secrets. We all do – it is what makes us human."

"Yes, we all have secrets," Rager thought, "and some more so than others. Some we bury so far down that we hope to forget about them."

He thought of Bristol and the shantytown. Windsor House seemed to be heading in the same direction. He asked Father Benoît about the nun's comments on the residential schools. "Father, Sister Brunelle mentioned the residential schools in her letter. She wrote that children were abused. Is that true?"

"Yes, it is true. Over the years I encouraged the parents to send their children to the residential schools, but when I heard their stories, I felt remorse. What we did to those innocent children was a great sin. I confronted my bishop, but he denied the stories. At the time I had no alternative but to believe what he said, but over the years I came to realize that he was lying. Let me say to you that those who have wronged so many will face a higher judgement when they die. No one – not even a bishop or a pope – can escape their sins. We are all sinners, either in thought or deed. They, too, will face a final day of judgement, as will you and I, Monsieur."

He reached over and placed his hand on Rager's shoulder. "You know that Sister Brunelle is no longer a nun. She lives in Toronto and works in a women's shelter. Someday you should talk to her. She was a good woman with a good heart – in French, we say 'un bon coeur.' She also had a good sense of humour. She told me once that everything could always be worse. I asked her how. She said we could all be dead." The priest laughed, and it seemed to break the awful mood of sadness.

Chapter 3
A BROKEN SPIRIT

(1)

They were camped across the lake with their small pup tent well hidden behind a wall of trees. He peered through a pair of binoculars and could see the Otter tied to the dock and the pilot waiting for a passenger. She cooked fish stew and Bannock over a Coleman stove and began to sing:

> I feel so bad I've got a worried mind
> I'm so lonesome all the time
> Since I left my baby behind on Blue Bayou
> Saving nickels, saving dimes, working until
> the sun don't shine
> Looking forward to happier times on
> Blue Bayou…

"Please stop singing," he said. "I can't concentrate."
"It's a beautiful song and I like to sing," she said.
"I don't feel like listening to your singing – sometimes, yes, but not now, so please stop."

Dorothy stopped singing and began to sulk.

Luke continued to peer through the binoculars until Rager arrived and boarded the plane. "Good, he's leaving. I don't have to answer any more questions. What does he know, or what does he think he knows? Nothing," he thought.

The plane began to taxi and took to the air. He stopped peering through the binoculars and began to drink the homebrew and smoke some weed. He could drink endlessly – alcohol seemed to have no detrimental effect on his ability to think – and the weed only freed his mind. He lay down on the ground and began to dream.

In memory he sees the white, oblong building, the ugly windows, the long corridors with crucifixes and images of saints on walls, a pantheon of the holy dead, and the dormitory where the children slept – the small bodies lying like soldiers going off to war in bunk beds, tiered one on top of the other – the dormitory that was never completely dark; even at night when the children slept, there was always a hall light casting a dark shadow. The priest stood over him "Are you sleeping, my child?" he asked. "Do not worry. I am here...remember, I am always here." The priest was young. His voice was tender and he smelled of lavender soap. He rested his hand against Luke's cheek.

"No, Father, I'm not sleeping," he replied.

"Then come, my son, come with me. I have something to show you." The priest took him by the hand and led him away. "Do not make a sound, child. Do not make a sound."

He was eight when the priest took him to the bedroom, fondled him, and raped him. After that, there were no secrets. He could never understand why he was chosen – *why me?* he wondered. There was no answer.

"Luke, do you want supper?" Dorothy asked.

"No! I'm not hungry."

"It's good fish stew," she said.

"No! Leave me alone."

As he lay on the ground she walked up to him, bent down onto the ground, and touched his face. "Luke, please eat something."

"No."

"Please, for me?"

"Go away!" he said.

"I don't want to go away."

"Then stay – stay." She stared at Luke's face; his eyes were closed and his face pained. She bent down and gave him a kiss. "My love, why are you always so unhappy?"

"You talk silly, Dorothy – I'm not unhappy and I'm not your love."

"You could be."

"No – not ever. We fuck, that's all we do. Just leave me alone!"

She went back to the Coleman stove and continued to stir the stew. She wore jeans, a man's heavy shirt, and rubber wading boots. She stared at Luke and smiled, thinking that he might marry her. "I wish I were smart," she said. "I would be rich and take care of everyone – and you especially. I would buy us a beautiful house, maybe in Winnipeg or Thunder Bay. We would have children and they would grow up to be strong and beautiful. We would be happy, all of us, living together."

He raised his head from the ground. "But you aren't very smart, Dorothy, and you never will be. It's not your fault. That's just the way it is. Some people are smart and others are not, some people are rich and others are poor, and some people are good looking and some are ugly. You just never know the way the dice are going to fall; you just never know. For us, our fate is to lie here, hiding behind trees."

"I know," she said. It was true that she was not very smart. She often felt like a child.

He drank more of the homebrew and smoked the rest of the weed. The homebrew was never as satisfying as the Seagram's Five Stars whiskey, but he would arrange for a charter in a day or two. When it came, he would drink the whiskey very slowly, listen to music, smoke weed, and laugh until there was nothing left to drink but homebrew. The band office could wait, the work could wait, and the world could wait. There was nothing urgent in the village. The empty houses and buildings were everywhere. They said, "Leave and don't come back."

Every summer Luke had begged his father not to send him to the residential school, but every summer his father did. "The government tells us you have to go, Luke," his father said. "They say you need to be educated. Father Benoît says so too, so you have to go." But then he was fondled and raped and, in a way, murdered. One summer he ran away into the forest, but his father found him and took him back. "Luke, you have to go; we have no choice.

You will thank me when you are old." But then he was fondled and raped and, in a way, murdered.

Dorothy stirred the stew and began to sing:

I feel so bad I've got a worried mind
I'm so lonesome all the time
Since I left my baby behind on Blue Bayou
Saving nickels, saving dimes, working until
the sun don't shine
Looking forward to happier times on
Blue Bayou…

"Why do you keep on singing the same song?" Luke asked.

"I like to sing. Besides, you're my baby."

"If you say so, Dorothy, but I'm not anything, not to anyone."

"Yes, you are, Luke. You're my baby." She loved to think of him as her husband, to think of just the two of them against the world. She lived in her own fantasy world that no one could touch.

Luke walked over to her. "Look at me, look into my eyes," he said.

She looked into his eyes.

"Listen to me, Dorothy. I was married once, but never again. Do you understand? I'll never marry you."

"Yes, baby, if you say so."

She removed the fish stew and Bannock from the stove, filled two bowls, and placed one on the ground next to him. "Here, my love, eat some stew. I'm going to read." She went to the tent, lay down on a sleeping bag, and began to read a fashion magazine. She marked the images she planned to cut out and glue into a scrapbook. He watched her through the tent flap – a child who would never be a grown woman.

The residential school building was always cold, even colder than the frozen winter ground. Even when he first arrived in late August, even then, lying in a bunk bed, alone, staring up at the ceiling, it was cold. He remembered the nuns yelling at him to not speak Ojibwa. He remembered a boy being strapped in front of the others as an example when he spoke back. He remembered another boy who had run away being beaten and locked in a room and then being strapped in front of the others. He remembered how they buried children, how they lied and told everyone that it was the sickness that killed them when it was the loneliness, beatings, and the priest that killed them. He remembered the sound of the ringing bells telling him when to wake, wash, eat, pray, go to class, and sleep. He remembered that some of the children said they would become nuns and priests but none ever did – not one. They all left or disappeared, and those that left were often changed forever, as though infected by a virus. He knew that he, too, was infected with the virus and kept it buried, hidden away, so no one would know that he was infected.

He peered through the binoculars. He could see the church and mission house on the small island and wished they could be burned to the ground. Only then would the wilderness creep back; only then would the church disappear.

He walked over to the campfire, picked up a hot, burning stick, and burned one of the warts on his fingers. He did this again on another finger until there were two burn marks, two black pieces of dead skin. It gave him pleasure to hurt himself. He was already dead.

Across the lake, Brother André rang the church bells. *Clang…Clang…Clang…Clang.* The sound reminded Luke of the building where they slept in bunks like small soldiers going off to war. He remembered praying to his father in the night, all alone, a small boy lying in bed waiting for the priest. "Father, help me! Save me! Please take me away from this evil place!" But there was no answer; not one sound, not until the priest appeared and whispered, "Come, my child, come with me."

He suddenly began to laugh – it was a hard, frightening laugh.

"Are you alright, baby?" Dorothy asked from the tent.

"Yes, I'm fine; I'll come to you later."

He peered through the binoculars. He could see two elders walking to church, a man and a woman. "Stubborn old goats who crawl to their graves, still believing in a God who doesn't exist. So stupid, more stupid than anything," he thought. "Stupid old fools…Stupid old fools."

Chapter 4
MARIE

Marie Brunelle was a small, sturdy woman with short blond hair and deep blue eyes who walked with her shoulders straight up and pushed back. She had grown up in Sherbrooke, Quebec; a young French-Canadian girl who often wore a blue kerchief over her blond hair as she ran out to greet people, "Bienvenue! Bienvenue!" People would yell back after her, "Marie! Marie!" Her name was full of joy and happiness, like the pure spring air or the bubbling brook near the shore of Lake Memphremagog, not far from Owl's Head Mountain.

The presence of Marie Brunelle was no longer felt in Windsor House. How she gave of herself, listening to what people had to say and answering their deepest questions as best she could. No, it was never easy to hear the pain in someone's voice as they begged for an answer, asking her what it all meant, and why me? After writing her letter to David Stewart, copied to Mr. Reed, Marie had had enough and left the village. It was harder to leave the Sisters of

Charity; and hardest of all to tell Mother Superior that she no longer believed in the Catholic church, a church that had destroyed so many lives, she said. "The young priest in the residential school raped the children, Mother Superior, and he was not alone. How many lives were destroyed? How many others are being destroyed as we speak?"

"If what you say is true, Sister Marie, then they will answer to God."

"What about here on Earth?"

"We are not the police."

"Who are we?"

"We give comfort to the poor and those who are lost. We save souls. We give hope," she answered.

"I need more than platitudes, Mother Superior." And so, Marie left.

Marie Brunelle came from a large family in the Eastern Townships of Quebec. She had gone to university to study philosophy before obtaining a Masters of Social Work. She spent a year in Paris, mostly drinking, making love, and reading novels, before joining the Sisters of Charity as a novice and then becoming a nun. She felt at home in the Catholic church – its liturgy, hymns, and sacraments – and the friendship of other women who gave of themselves, who were, in a way, each other. She had no doubt that she was meant to be a nun: not a wife, not a mother, but a servant of God. What she discovered in Windsor House were lies, and it was the lies and the protection of monsters that led her to leave the order, and then the Catholic church. She never told anyone else except Mother

Superior that the Catholic church was a lie, everything about the church was a lie, because it protected monsters.

When Marie showed up at the women's shelter in Toronto, she told them she wanted to help, and they hired her as a counsellor. For her, the church was gone. She would carve out a new path, and a new life, and she let her hair grow longer and longer until she felt free.

Part Three

Chapter 1

LIMBO

(1)

In early October, the days became shorter, the wind colder, and the leaves began to pile high on the ground. In the fly-in villages when the lakes and rivers began to freeze, an elder would often drop a pouch of tobacco into the water and offer a few words of comfort – "I will see you again next spring old friend. Until then, sleep well." Then, over a three-week period, the wind would move at night from place to place, quietly whispering, "Change," and then, suddenly, in the morning there appeared a fine, thin layer of ice, a frozen mirror, a magnificent wonder.

The Nakina Indian Affairs district supervisor of construction was a man in his early fifties who drank heavily, smoked, and ate far too much for his own good. Freddy Birch's squat body, blood-shot eyes, drooping eyelids, and bulbous vein-covered nose were all too evident. As a result, he suffered from lumbago, sciatica, and high blood pressure, and often called in sick. "My lumbago is acting up again," he would tell the receptionist. He was also temperamental, easily agitated, and a walking 'time bomb' who often yelled at his wife about the escalating price of the wholesale food supplies that he ordered for her convenience store on Main Street – "How are we expected to earn a profit when they're milking us dry?" he would scream. It was, therefore, understandable that Freddy Birch felt more than justified in making a few extra dollars by soliciting a bribe and awarding Mensen a fuel delivery contract that was a much higher cost to the agency than the Northwest Company bid. So what if an Indian chief complained that fuel prices would climb and cost the villagers more, it was all government money? "It's none of any chief's business," Freddy thought.

His assistant, Olaf Jehkinen, was a tall muscular Finlander in his late thirties who drank alcohol at every opportunity – whether in Grayson, the Indian villages, Thunder Bay, or Helsinki where he visited his grandparents. Olaf did all the minor repairs in the nine district Indian Affairs schools and teacherages, and ran a side business selling aluminum boats, canoes, and outboard motors. He was the father of five children with numerous responsibilities far more important than worrying about what a chief might or might not think. He, too, felt that awarding a fuel contract to Mensen was more than justified.

The two men occupied a large cubicle in the front office that was always crowded with equipment, blueprints, stacked messages, and bottles of liquor hidden away in desk drawers, and were inseparable as much as Tweedledum and Tweedledee.

Today, more so than most days, Mr. Reed was annoyed with Freddy, not only because the supervisor had been sick for a week, but also because Freddy's decision to award Mensen the fuel contract was causing Mr. Reed misery. The Northwest Company wanted to know why they were passed over on the fuel contract. "You better have a good reason or we're taking this to my boss, and he's got a lot more leverage than I do," the Northwest manager had threatened over the phone.

They sat in the district manager's office. Mr. Reed was visibly worried – his white hair was ruffled and his face pale. "Why did you award the fuel contract to Mensen, Freddy?" he asked. The supervisor was unsure of how to respond, so he shifted his squat body nervously. He had a bad hangover – sipping cognac in bed was not what his doctor prescribed for lumbago. He needed a drink but decided he would wait and later slip away to the Canadian Legion for a few cold beers.

"You have to keep in mind, Bob, that awarding a fuel contract is a complex matter. You have to take into account not only the price of the fuel, but also the cost of transportation and the level of service. Mensen gives us *good* service - not perfect, but *good*." He emphasized the word *good* as though Mensen's service was a perfect peach.

"Forget the 'good service' spiel. You agreed to pay Mensen ten percent more than the Northwest! Why? Why did you do that? Why didn't you at least split the contract between the two companies? Goddammit, Freddy, we're going to have another complaint sitting on my desk." Mr. Reed was annoyed. Even though he was dozy, his tone whiny – the sort that a servile clerk might use – his use of profanity was unusual. From a normally polite man, it sounded obscene.

"Well, Bob, if you split the contract between companies, all you have are two companies flying around. No, it makes more sense to give it all to Mensen. He can make more money and give us *good* service. Makes sense, doesn't it – *good* service?" Freddy didn't wait for a reply. "I think so. Besides, the Northwest manager is rude and calls me a drunk and a whole lot worse things. Why should I have to put up with his insults? How would you like it?"

"Well, I don't drink, Freddy. Maybe the occasional glass of wine or port, but not much else."

"Anyway, I've had to cut back on the drinking because of my doctor's orders. I have to stay healthy. Besides, the last time we used the Northwest they were slow in delivery – too slow for me, anyway." Birch mumbled a few words about aircraft and times and the need to be prompt and polite and do what he said, whenever it suited him. He was, after all, the contractor.

Mr. Reed was not convinced. "Jesus, Freddy…Jesus, you should know better." The words coming out of the district manager's mouth sounded weak and pathetic. If Mr. Reed had any authority over the supervisor, it had been lost a long time ago. Mr. Reed looked at Freddy and thought, "How much longer must I endure this misery?"

Then he said aloud, "All right, Freddy, have it your own way. Let Mensen have the contract, but I want you to write up the rationale for awarding the contract to a company with a higher bid because of good service. Can you please to do that one thing for me?"

"No problem, Bob. I'll draft a memo to file and sign it. Happy?"

"I suppose it will have to do." Mr. Reed accepted the reality that the contract had been awarded.

"Bob, what do you have to worry about? You'll be gone in three months."

"I know, but still…"

"Still what?"

"Nothing."

"Good."

The supervisor would earn a free winter trip to the Caribbean where the rum was cheap, and no one would be the wiser. Indian Affairs would pay much more for heating the school and government buildings in five villages, leaving less to spend on other needs, and the villagers would pay more for gasoline for their snowmobiles and outboard engines, but this meant nothing to him. There was no connection – only his benefit. Freddy left the district manager's office, and hobbled down the stairs over to the Legion. He always needed a drink to celebrate a victory over the cowardly, pathetic district manager.

Mr. Reed read Rager's Windsor House report. It was an ambitious plan that offered numerous benefits – these were all listed: a police presence that would reduce the violence and drinking; repairs and re-opening of the school that would draw villagers back to the village; the opening and subsidizing of the sawmill – it would result in the use of a local source of wood to repair houses, reduce cost, and create seasonal employment and income; and the establishment of a five-fly-in village-owned development corporation to own and operate the agency camps – in so doing, it would place control of the camps in the hands of those most affected. Rager also recommended that the agency contract a consulting firm to develop a business plan outlining: markets, management, required capital, financing, and five-year financial projections. He included an implementation plan with a timeline.

After reading the report, Mr. Reed concluded that it was a far too ambitious plan and, as he often did in similar situations, decided not to forward the report to anyone. "When Gordon is district manager, he can decide what to do," Mr. Reed thought to himself. "Windsor House can wait – three months won't make a bit of difference. Besides, the region is likely to say no to most of the recommendations. How can we force the province to station a police officer in one village and not the others? Well, we can't, and that's the end of it. As for a development corporation, who's going to fund a corporation run by Indians with no business experience? Absolutely no one. It's just too much to ask, at least for now. Perhaps it would be feasible in ten or twenty years, when the Indians are more educated. Perhaps then, but not now. I also don't know why he didn't include a small craft shop in the report, something modest, simple, and easy to fund."

As for Rager's recommendation that the agency follow up with the chief and council's desire to relocate the village in the long-term, Mr. Reed decided it was beyond his or Rager's purview. Besides, where would the money come from?

On top of all this, Mr. Reed decided not to say anything to Rager. "Why tell the man anything? All he'll do is argue. He has no sense of proportion, no ability to compromise or see the big picture. Besides, he needs to learn that sometimes you can't do everything. I should never have asked him to develop an action plan. He's completely out of control."

Mr. Reed operated like a sleeping lizard that never really wakes – it just lies comfortably in a quiet hollow or a deep bush where it can curl up unnoticed. He had been like that all his life – a government official who did as little as possible to help others. There was only one outstanding issue, and it concerned the lack of a Manpower Local Initiative Project (LIP) report. He therefore took his time in writing Rager a memo saying he was disappointed that no information on the project had been collected: "John, I am disappointed about the lack of an LIP report. You were in the village and could easily have taken the time to collect the information. These are the sorts of things we can't let slip."

When Mr. Reed left the office early, he wondered where Freddy and Olaf had disappeared to. Their cubicle was empty. But then, it really didn't matter. When it came right down to it, nothing really mattered – except his own reputation. Like a sliding lizard, he hoped that no one noticed him slipping out of the office, quietly, through the back door, and down the back stairs.

Chapter 2
A DISTRICT MEETING

(1)

On Tuesday, November 9, 1976, the Nakina Indian Affairs district office held its biannual district meeting. In attendance were eight district chiefs and eight band managers, with Windsor House the only village not represented; neither its chief nor Luke saw the logic in attending a meeting where everything had already been decided. Also in attendance were four district agency officials: Gordon Hughes, district manager-designate, who served as facilitator; the supervisor of education, who had no intention of reopening the Windsor House school until there was assurance that a police officer would be stationed in the village; Olaf, standing in for Freddy, who was absent because of his lumbago; and the very sweet, chatty, ineffective supervisor of social services. Including an interpreter for two of the chiefs, there were twenty-three people gathered in the Grayson Hotel conference room with the objective of reviewing and discussing the already-approved Indian Affairs district budget for the 1977-78 fiscal year.

Following the opening prayer, Gordon outlined the district budget, which was broken down into housing, education, training, recreation, capital infrastructure, social assistance, and economic development. As he gave his overview, a number of participants complained about the lack of spending. On the topic of capital infrastructure, none of the fly-in villages had water or sewage. On the topic of housing, all of the chiefs complained about crowded houses – as one of the chiefs said pointedly, "If you want to drive people crazy, crowd ten of them into a two-bedroom house." On the topic of economic development, one of the band administrators pointed out that only three percent of the total district budget was allocated to this area in what was already a poor district budget – the band administrator commented, "Economic development supports self-reliance and independence from government and should have more than three percent. The way you've set it up, we'll always be poor, always rely on welfare, and always suck on the government tit. I guess that's why you set it up that way."

Gordon replied, "Well, it's not up to me to decide how much gets spent on economic development. I agree, though, that more should be spent. I will discuss it with Stewart."

The band administrator was not happy and doubted that anything would change, but he had no recourse but to sit and listen.

The exchange established a pattern: whenever an unpleasant issue appeared, Gordon responded that he would take it up with David Stewart, the regional director general in Toronto who had never once attended a district meeting, travelled to any of the district villages, or knew any of the chiefs.

Gordon went on to say that the district budget was a "fixed pie" – by that, he meant the budget was fixed by those more powerful than him and so was out of his control. This fixed pie, this very limited fixed pie, was divided among the nine villages, either by population, which no one could know with absolute certainty, or need, which everyone had in abundance. When Gordon said "out of my control," the interpreter winked to everyone. Gordon was following a long tradition of government officials blaming a superior for the state of affairs. This practice went back to 1905 when the James Bay Treaty, or Treaty Nine, was signed and government officials continued the practice, believing the chiefs were unaware of what was happening: government officials pretending to be upset and disturbed, when in fact they cared not a whit.

During the meeting it also became apparent that Gordon had very little appreciation of Treaty Nine. One of the chiefs remarked, "The only good thing about Treaty Nine is that it acknowledges we are a sovereign nation. Do you understand, Gordon, it's crown to crown, nation to nation?"

Instead of acknowledging that he understood, Gordon replied that as far as he was concerned, the only nation that had signed the treaty was Canada and the only crown was that of Queen Elizabeth II.

Among the village delegates – a group who accepted that Indian Affairs officials controlled the budget and would dictate what they were to receive – was the young, often hostile Otter Falls chief. Elijah Wapoose had very deep concerns with everything that Gordon said, so much so that he was prepared to openly challenge him. Elijah had once stood with a rifle on the Otter Falls community dock to prevent a chartered plane filled with district officials from disembarking and holding a public meeting. In his opinion they were only going to make empty promises to the villagers. The officials finally left, upset, nervous, and barely able to speak about how a chief holding a rifle had forcibly prevented them from holding a public meeting. It was months before any district official was able to enter the village.

When it seemed appropriate, Elijah spoke loud and clear. "Gordon, you're the biggest liar I know! You told me, in person, face to face, that we would be getting three houses in the new fiscal year, and now you tell me we get nothing. You told me we would be getting a recreation center in two years, and now you tell me it's five or ten years away. You told me the department was planning to start building sewage lines and a piped water line, and now it's not even mentioned. All you ever do is lie. At least Reed, the old fart, would just say he didn't know and wouldn't promise anything. But with you, it's always saying one thing and then changing the story, using bullshit words like 'fiscal constraint' and 'we all have to do our part' and 'it's not up to me' and all that other crap to hide what's already been decided: we don't get what we need, what we were promised, and we never will. You're a fucking liar, just like everyone else in Indian Affairs. We should all get up and leave!" He glared at Gordon, leaving no doubt that he was deadly serious.

At that point Gordon became visibly upset. He replied, "Elijah, I think you should watch what you're saying. After all, it's not my place to decide how much money to spend; it's the regional office that makes those decisions, and they get their orders from Ottawa. I'm just the messenger boy. My God, if I had my way, every village in the district would get more houses, a recreation center, sewage and water lines, even a water treatment plant, and everything else." This from the same man who had suggested to Mr. Reed that the villages should be amalgamated into larger centers to reduce cost.

Elijah replied, "Well then, Gordon, why don't you do something instead of caving in to your bosses – why don't you say something?"

"Oh, but I will, Elijah. After the meeting finishes, I plan to phone Stewart to let him know how you all feel. That I promise! Certainly – why wouldn't I?"

But Elijah knew he would do no such thing. Why would Gordon upset a man who held his future in his hands?

"Because no one wants to hear it and you know it. So, you lie."

The interpreter didn't bother to translate the last word because everyone in the room knew what it meant.

Not missing an opportunity, Elijah raised another issue. "By the way, Gordon, why is Freddy not at this meeting? After all, he awarded a fuel contract to Mensen that was worth far more than the Northwest bid. It means a lot less funding for us, a lot more that we as a people will have to pay for gasoline, and a lot more profit for Mensen. How does that work? How did Freddy decide to award a contract to a company that submitted a much higher bid? Can you explain that to me? I really would like to know." Elijah knew far more than he let on.

Gordon grew more nervous. He could barely speak. All he could think was, "Freddy made such a stupid decision – and for what, a trip to the Caribbean?" He replied, "I'll look into it, Elijah. Let's not talk about it here."

Then another chief spoke up about always being kept in the dark. The awarding of the contract to Mensen was just one more example of how the district office operated.

Then another chief asked, "What's the point of holding a meeting to talk about budgets when you guys make all the decisions? All we do is sit here and listen to you spout off about handing out bits of money when we need millions. You know we represent poor communities. You know we have nothing like any other communities across the province. You know we lack housing, education facilities, infrastructure, and goddammit, everything else. You know the government has no intention of investing to give us what we need – and yet it's the government who placed us in this situation. You know all that, and yet you do nothing. Messenger boy, my ass. You represent what is the worst thing about Indian Affairs, you defend what the government does. And now, Jesus Christ, what I hear from Elijah is that you're screwing us over by giving Mensen a contract that's only going to steal more money from our people. You're all a bunch of hypocrites! And you, Gordon, if I have to hear you spout one more time that it's not up to you, I'll slap that mouth of yours." The chief was a powerful man and left no doubt that he could easily handle Gordon.

At that point a deep silence came over the room. A chief had spoken the truth. Gordon looked around, not certain of how to respond. Finally, nervously, he spoke. "It was Freddy who made the decision to award the fuel contract I had nothing to do with it – not a thing. But I'll look into it. If there's a problem, I'll fix it."

"Again, more bullshit!" Elijah said. "Freddy gets free trips to the Caribbean and should be fired!"

"You have no proof," Gordon replied.

"No proof? He bragged about it to the fishing guides."

"So, you say."

"Fuck you!"

Gordon offered no reply. There was nothing to say.

The exchange between the two men set the tone for the rest of the meeting. Clearly to everyone in the room, the district manager-designate was no better than Mr. Reed – in fact, he was far worse. At noon they broke for lunch. Elijah decided to spend the rest of his time drinking and retreated to the Main Hotel. After lunch, only three of the chiefs and two of the band administrators bothered to return to the meeting. Gordon, however, revealed just how little he understood of the situation when he raised the likelihood of future budget cuts. "We can anticipate that cuts will be coming," he said, "so we need to plan."

"How do we know that cuts are coming?" one of the band administrators asked.

"We don't, but I think it's inevitable."

"Why don't we plan for an increase?"

Gordon stayed silent.

The next day only one of the band administrators bothered to show up. At that point Gordon cancelled the meeting. Nonetheless, later that day he phoned Stewart and reported. "David, we had an excellent meeting. Everyone said what they wanted, and everyone was in agreement on the allocation of funding. Oh, there were a few naysayers – there always are in these sorts of meetings – but I would consider the meeting, at the very least, a success."

(2)

When Freddy heard that the Otter Falls chief had accused him of taking bribes, he was furious. "Who the fuck does Elijah think he is, questioning my authority?" he said to Olaf. And so, when he heard later that the young chief was drinking alone in the Main Hotel bar, he decided to act swiftly. As he put it to Olaf, "We need to give that little fucker a lesson he won't easily forget."

"I never did like the little prick," Olaf replied.

The Main Hotel bar was an older establishment, reminiscent of a much earlier time when Grayson operated with three thriving gold mines, when miners and bars were everywhere. But now, like the town itself, the bar was almost empty. Besides the bartender watching a hockey game on television, there were only four customers. One of them was Elijah sitting alone at a table, drunk and belligerent. The bartender had warned him a number of times to "stop mouthing off about Indian Affairs."

Freddy approached Elijah. "I heard you complained about me in the meeting yesterday. Why'd you do that, Elijah? Why'd you open your mouth and say things you know nothing about?"

Elijah could barely speak. "U...steal...Freddy...u steal!"

"I don't steal."

"Yeah...u...do."

"Can I buy you a drink?"

"Fuck...off!"

Freddy and Olaf retreated to another table. They waited until the bar closed and everyone left. Then they followed the chief as he stumbled down Main Street unaware that he was being followed. They followed him until he walked into a back alley to relieve himself. "Do you think he sees us?" Olaf whispered.

"No, he's too drunk. He can barely stand. You go first. You take him down, Olaf. Hurt him, hurt him bad, make him cry, make him bleed."

"This will be fun," Olaf replied.

The Finlander came up from behind with his right hand already balled into a fist. "Hey, Chief, we need to talk."

"What...the..."

The chief never did finish the sentence when Olaf punched him hard in the face. Elijah swung back, missed, and Olaf punched him twice until he fell to the ground, grunted, and passed out. At that point, Freddy ran up and they dragged the fallen chief down into the alley. "You hold him and make sure he doesn't move," Freddy instructed. Olaf held the unconscious man onto the pavement. Freddy stood over Elijah and struck his face, blow after blow. Then he kicked him in the head before Olaf took over, kicked him in the groin, and punched him until he heard his nose snap. They left him unconscious, gurgling in a pool of blood. "It sure feels good to beat an Indian. God, it feels good," Freddy said.

Elijah didn't wake until the early morning. When he did, he could barely remember what had happened. His face was swollen, an eye shut, his lower lip split open where a front tooth was broken, and his clothes were torn and stained in blood. He was barely able to stand, but somehow managed. Slowly, he began to walk out of the alley and onto Main Street.

When two Ontario Provincial Police officers driving a cruiser saw a beaten-up Indian man stumbling along Main Street, they didn't hesitate to make an arrest. They took him to the police station, booked him, and threw him into a holding cell.

Elijah was left alone for two days and two nights. He was given food and water, but no one bothered to send for a nurse or a doctor to examine his physical condition. The OPP sergeant on duty said, "Don't give him anything – no painkillers, no aspirin, nothing. He needs to learn a lesson about not fucking with people."

No one bothered to take anything Elijah said seriously – least of all his claim that two Indian Affairs district officials had beaten him up in a back alley. When he said that he was the Otter Falls chief and deserved better treatment, the OPP sergeant said, "Well, Chief, you need to earn *my* respect!" And that was the end of it.

(3)

Rager was angry, but not surprised, when he heard about how the district meeting had ended. More than anyone in the district office, he understood the world the government had created for Indians. "The government built the villages by providing housing, schools, and nursing stations. They encouraged the Indians to settle into the villages, providing them with just enough welfare and make-work programs to exist. But the houses were poorly built, the schools under-funded, and none of the fly-in villages ever got sewage lines, piped water, or anything else that anyone would consider basic services.

"With economic development, Indians Affairs invests so little it's almost a joke. If it were a game of monopoly and the government was the banker, at the start of the game the Indian player is given almost no money to play with, so by the end of the game, guess who owns Park Place, Boardwalk, and most of the other properties? It sure isn't the Indian player. Not in this district, not in northwestern Ontario, not where the white business operators, white corporations, white family trusts – the whites, period – own the sawmills, mines, airlines, construction companies, and everything else. You could almost say the government set up a system to keep the whites in control and the Indians subservient. It's no different than the system of Apartheid in South Africa.

"Most Canadians don't know anything about Indian history. Children have been forced to attend residential schools, torn away from families, with the government telling them they had to go. If the Indians move to the towns and cities, they often can't get work or housing, and there's a good chance that Children's Aid will take their children and place them in foster care."

As for himself, he felt lost. "What am I going to do?", he wondered. " I've lost my wife and son. I don't have much to live for – just the work of helping a few remote Indian villages free themselves from the yoke of government. Maybe I should quit. Maybe I could do international work for CIDA?" The Canadian International Development Agency had been formed in 1968 to assist developing countries. But Rager felt he had done so very little. "Why bother with another country? Running away solves nothing." He concluded: "I need to ride this out."

That was what he thought about as he waited for a response to his Windsor House report, unaware of what had transpired in a back alley late one night.

(4)

The stairway leading up to the reception area in the Nakina district office was always cold and unwelcoming – even more so if you were an Indian pulling yourself up by the railing. The chief's face was hardly recognizable and his groin was in agonizing pain. After leaving the police holding cell, Elijah had hobbled over to the hospital emergency room, where a nurse had stitched an eye and given him Tylenol, but no doctor had bothered to exam him to confirm if there was any internal bleeding, or set his nose. He was simply another Indian recuperating from a drunken fight.

When the receptionist saw him, her immediate reaction was one of fear. Should she call the police, or run to see Mr. Reed? But when Elijah asked to see Rager, common sense prevailed, and she informed the commerce officer. "John, there's a badly beaten Indian man who wants to see you. His name is Elijah Wapoose and he says that he's the Otter Falls chief. Let me know if you want me to call the OPP?"

Rager knew Elijah. On his first visit to Otter Falls, they had discussed starting the development corporation. Elijah felt it would enable the villages to finally take their place in the region's economy – as he put it, "It's the only way we're going to get ahead in this capitalist world, the only way. Otherwise, nothing will change."

Rager replied to the receptionist, "Don't call the police. I know Elijah. Something terrible must have happened." When he saw the young chief – his face black and blue, an eye stitched and weeping, his front tooth missing and a broken nose – he was dumbfounded. "My God, what happened, Elijah?"

The chief was bitter. He spoke slowly. "Freddy and Olaf did this to me. I spoke up at the district meeting about Freddy taking bribes from Mensen. They followed me out of the Main Hotel bar the following night and beat me up in an alley. When the police saw me, they threw me into jail. I was kept in jail for two days before I was released and went to the hospital." He took a breath – the pain on his beaten face was all too evident. "Everyone knows Freddy takes bribes and that the commerce officer before you took bribes. Reed, Gordon, the supervisors, they all pretend that nothing happens, but they all know. I know you don't take bribes, John, but those are the people you work with. That's the government – that's what they do. When they can't get their way, they beat you up."

"What can I do?" Rager asked.

"You can tell Reed that no one from the Indian Affairs district office is welcome in Otter Falls, not until Freddy and Olaf are arrested and charged."

"He might not do anything."

"Then I'll go public. I want everyone to know how we're treated up here. How officials take bribes and steal when they're supposed to help. How a chief gets beaten up by Indian Affairs officials when he speaks up. How nothing gets done to change things. I need change for my people." Elijah began to shake uncontrollably. He reached out his hand to steady himself against the desk.

When he did, Rager reached over and placed his hand on the man's shoulder. "Believe me, Elijah, I'll do everything in my power to make it right. They won't get away with it. I promise you."

When the chief left, Rager went over to see Mr. Reed. The older man was almost asleep at his desk, within reach were a couple of marked-over travel magazines that had set him dreaming of Florida. He might easily have been a tourist in the departure lounge of an airport, waiting to board a flight. "Bob, we need to talk." And so began the first of Rager's bold steps.

Upon being told of the beating, Mr. Reed replied, "I already know about the incident. The OPP sergeant phoned me. Don't believe anything Elijah Wapoose tells you. He's a troublemaker and a liar – of course, they all lie, you can't believe anything an Indian tells you. I also spoke with Freddy and Olaf. True enough, they were in the Main Hotel bar, but they never sat together, and they certainly never beat up Elijah. Bottom line, it's his word against theirs, and there are two of them. I think you know where I'm going with this. Elijah made it all up and someone else beat him up. You know, of course, that Elijah once held a rifle to a number of our officials and prevented them from holding a public meeting in Otter Falls. The man's crazy, dangerous, and capable of anything. Don't believe a word he says. Leave it alone – just let it go."

"What about the Mensen fuel contract – why was it awarded to Mensen when the Northwest put in a much lower bid?"

"Service. The company gives better service."

"Really?"

"You might not think so, but yes, they offer much better service."

"Bob, you know that's a lie. Mensen got the contract because Freddy takes bribes!"

Mr. Reed looked over at the travel magazines – the sandy beach, the women in skimpy bikinis. He could smell the ocean breeze. He gave a weak, insipid smile.

Rager left the office angry and disgusted.

The older man with the dopey eyes got up and walked out of the office and onto Main Street. It was a sunny day and he felt very much alive. What did he care about Elijah Wapoose or any Indian? Mr. Reed was a strange creature who moved without really moving – sliding along, close

to the ground, hiding, and still, somehow, very much alive
and not quite dead.

Chapter 3:
TORONTO REGIONAL OFFICE

(1)

The Toronto regional office was on the sixth floor of a downtown building, close enough to a subway station to make travel to and from the office efficient and affordable. All in all, it was a good location: a large government office, centrally located, close to shops, restaurants, and a municipal park, and relatively easy to reach. Everyone who worked in the office knew this, from the lowest-paid clerk to the highest-ranking official. No one ever thought of relocating the office. It was, therefore, as permanent as the provincial legislature, Nathan Philips Square, or the newly built CN Tower. It was also functional and highly efficient, or so it seemed to the Department of Public Works officials who had designed the office. But they had their own ideas about function and office traffic flow.

In the beginning the office was comprised of small, separate offices, each with a desk and filing cabinet, but this proved unworkable as the number of staff increased exponentially and new hires began sharing offices and spilling out into hallways. The solution to the problem was to re-design the office into a large, open-concept space with colour-coded cubicles for different departments, signs letting visitors know who was who, and four glass cubicles for the regional superintendents of economic development, capital projects, local government, and education. The regional director general was the only one with a spacious corner office.

Everything seemed to be working well, except for one major problem: as democratic as it seemed, the open concept lacked privacy. As staff increased, people crowded into cubicles and everyone could hear what everyone else was saying. Telephone calls, private and otherwise, were overhead, often leading to disputes until staff began to meet outside in restaurants and parks to talk about sensitive matters – promotions, who was sleeping with who, and the conflicts that affect any large group of people crowded together. Soon it was not a very joyful place, but a conflict-ridden office.

The HR Manager had tried to correct the problem with late Friday afternoon parties, social gatherings, and the celebration of staff birthdays. Everyone was getting fat with cakes and pastries, but it never did get any better. In fact, over time the tension only got worse. People would yell at each other, throw things, scream – even the finance manager once had to be sent home for making threats to a junior female clerk about her inappropriate dress.

It was in this office that Rager waited patiently in the reception area to see Stephen Majors, the regional superintendent of economic development. The day before, he had driven to Thunder Bay and taken an evening flight to

Toronto. It was a miserable, uncomfortable hour-and-a-half flight on a crowded Air Canada jet passing over Lake Superior through thunderstorms, bouncing up and down between dark thundering clouds and flashes of lighting as it circled over Lake Ontario, ending with a landing in torrential downpour at the Toronto International Airport. Tired, nervous, and badly needing sleep, Rager had taken a shuttle downtown and, after a couple of drinks, fallen asleep in a room at the Holiday Inn. In the morning, after a quick shower and a cup of coffee, he had skipped breakfast and taken a taxi to the regional office. He was not very "up" for the meeting, but he knew that with Stephen, he would have to tell a convincing story.

A week earlier, Rager had phoned and spoken with the regional superintendent, telling him of the bribes and how two district officials had beaten up an Indian chief late at night in a dark alley. The regional superintendent was incredulous. "These are very serious accusations, John. You can't just say all this. You need proof," he said.

Rager replied, "I don't have proof, except for my own confirmation that the owner of the Mensen Air Charter Services Company, Teddy Mensen, did offer me bribes for the air service contract for the agency tourist camps, and Elijah told me that the district supervisor of construction, Freddy Birch, and his assistant, Olaf Jehkennen, beat him up for speaking up about Freddy taking bribes from Mensen for a fuel contract. But I'm telling you that the district office is run poorly, there is no accountability, staff pretty much do whatever they want, and corruption is rampant. Reed is an incompetent fool and might as well be asleep – did you know that he drives to Toronto every second month because he's afraid of flying?"

"No, I didn't. But I suppose that's his decision."

"All I'm saying is that he does nothing. He never visits the district villages and denies that officials take bribes, even though he knows they do. I'm telling you there has to be an accounting and some serious changes. How can we go into any district village if we allow this sort of stuff?

"There's also a letter to the regional director general from a Catholic nun, Sister Brunelle, outlining her experience in Windsor House – the terrible drinking and violence, school closure, poor housing, lack of infrastructure, and what she heard from villagers about district officials taking bribes. All the district chiefs know that my predecessor, Walt Cannon, also took bribes from Mensen – free trips to the Caribbean seems to be his preferred method. The practice of taking bribes has been going on for a long time.

"I also wrote a report outlining a plan to help Windsor House, but I haven't heard anything back from Reed. Has David Stewart raised the subject with you?"

"I know nothing of any nun's letter to David or a Windsor House report. So, to answer your question: No. I know nothing, and no one has said anything to me. But you better come down here so we can talk. Take the flight from Thunder Bay next Sunday and I'll see you Monday morning. I'm certain we can figure this out." Stephen added as a caution, "Don't get carried away. Remember, you're new to the agency. Making unfounded accusations could cause a lot of trouble."

And so, following these instructions, Rager drove to Thunder Bay on Sunday and took the evening flight to Toronto.

Stephen Majors knew very little about his new commerce officer – other than that he was thirty-six, divorced, held a commerce degree, a CGA, and had worked in Ottawa for different accounting firms. He also knew that Rager had relocated to Sioux Lookout to work for the Ontario Cooperative Development Association as a business advisor. All that was enough information to hire him without holding an in-person interview – a phone call and a few questions were all that was required. During the interview, Rager had said, "I want to help people who no one thinks about. I want to make a difference; it means a lot to me. I believe that economic development can help reduce dependency on government. I think I can help to make that happen." When Rager spoke, there was sincerity in his voice. Stephen thought he would make a fine replacement for Walt, who was lazy, a former bartender, and had done nothing to encourage economic development in the district. Stephen had learned that in the federal government it was almost impossible to fire anyone and, therefore, arranged for Walt's transfer. But to have his new commerce officer turn into a whistle-blower after six months was not what he expected.

As for Rager, he knew very few people in regional office. In many ways he felt like a stranger meeting someone he hardly knew, someone who stood over him like a stern judge.

Stephen Majors was a lanky, serious man who thought and acted conservatively, the sort who carried a lunch bag to work to save money, and from early spring to late fall pedaled a bicycle back and forth from his home in the Beaches to the regional office. On the street, he appeared more like a British public-school teacher pedaling to work than a government official. He was named after his father, Stephen Senior, but everyone in the family called him Sonny. Like his father, he held an engineering degree from the University of Toronto in addition to an MBA. His father had told him, "These days, there seem to be more and more people getting MBAs. In my day, you would learn business through experience, but I suppose now you need an MBA."

To everyone in the regional office, it was evident that Stephen was a hard-working government official. His cubicle was stacked with files and reports and everyday people could see his dedication to keeping the paper moving. Seven years earlier, Stephen had worked as a consultant with an international consulting firm, overseeing World Bank engineering projects in the Caribbean. But the work was stressful – for one thing, he was always under pressure to generate as many billable hours as possible – and unrewarding – he was often away from home for extended periods of time which eventually led him to leave the firm and seek employment with the federal government. Through old university friends, he secured a position as secretary to the Ontario Indian Affairs Small Business Loan Fund before being promoted to his current position, where he worked as hard as he could, thinking it was only a matter of time before the agency promoted him to regional director general. After all, David Stewart was a career academic on a two-year leave of absence to help the agency reorganize, with no long-term ambition to stay or seek a promotion.

Stephen led a pleasant life. He and his wife Catherine, a city librarian, would often walk on the boardwalk beside Lake Ontario. She too was comfortable in the work that allowed her to garden, take yoga lessons, and share quiet moments with old friends. The couple had no children – they had long ago decided that having children was something for other people. "The world is already over-populated. Why should we contribute to the problem?" Stephen said, and Catherine readily agreed. They could often be seen in the early morning heading off to work, a couple with bagged lunches pedaling down a quiet resi-dential street, waving to each other before parting, "See you later, honey!" each heading off in different directions.

Life smiled on Stephen. If he ever thought about Indian villages, it was to reflect on how they were impossible to repair – much like the businesses supported by the Indian Small Business Loan Fund, where seventy percent of loans were in arrears and the program was impossible to repair without an annual injection of funds. These were issues he had no answer to, so he stopped thinking about them. They were simply unsolvable problems – and there were so many unsolvable problems with Indians that it was just not worth thinking about.

When the two men met, Rager repeated what he had told the regional superintendent on the phone but took more time. "Stephen, let me tell you what it's been like since I first arrived in Grayson." He pointed to his predecessor's advice to take bribes. "On the first day that I showed up, Walt advised me to take bribes from Mensen. He said that everyone did and I should just go along with the practice. Of course, it was offensive and I told him, 'I don't take bribes.' The idea that Mensen gives 'better service' to the camps is a ruse to award him untendered contracts. Moreover, Reed has always known what was happening but has done nothing to stop the practice. Instead, he pretends that Mensen gives better service when no one knows what that means. Two months ago, I awarded the tourist camp contract to the Northwest Air Services Company because they submitted a much lower bid."

Stephen replied, "Why didn't you tell me?"

"Well, I am now."

"You better have your facts straight, because I transferred Walt to the Sioux Lookout district. If I had known he accepted bribes, I never would have offered him the position."

Rager pointed to Sister Brunelle's letter and what she had discovered in Windsor House: a village with a tortured history, and her accusation that district officials took bribes. He described Mr. Reed's reaction to the letter: his outright refusal to admit that anything was wrong, his fear that the letter might go public and lead to an inquiry, and his decision to send Rager into the village to develop an action plan. "Reed and the district supervisor of education have kept the village school closed for over a year because teachers don't want to work in a building with a broken furnace, broken furniture, and a lack of a permanent police presence, and these are things that Reed has done nothing to address. I did go to Windsor House. I met the chief and council, and I wrote a report with five recommendations, which I submitted to Reed in early October. He's probably sitting on it because I haven't heard a word out of him."

"I'm sorry to hear that you worked on something that has gone nowhere," Stephen replied. "Maybe the report got lost in the mail. You never know, these things do happen. We have so much paperwork passing through the regional office that it is often overwhelming." Stephen stared at the pile of paperwork lying on his desk. Some of the pile seemed to be teetering ready to fall. "My point is that you have to be careful about what you say."

Rager described Elijah showing up in his office, beaten up. "When I saw Elijah, I could hardly believe my eyes. His face was black and blue. He had an eye stitched, a broken front tooth, broken nose, and he could barely stand without shaking. The police had thrown him into jail because he was drunk. They kept him there for two days before he was released, not once bothering to send for a doctor. He was only treated at the hospital after his release. Elijah told me that no one is welcome in Otter Falls, not until Freddy and Olaf are arrested and charged. How long do you think we can last before the other villages start doing the same thing, telling us to keep out?"

Rager described Mensen as a bully and a racist – someone who supplied prostitutes and tried to intimidate people. He told him of the day when Mensen squeezed his neck so Rager would arrange to sell him the agency camps. "The man is dangerous and determined to get possession of the camps one way or another. He cares nothing about the villages. This is the way he operates. He seeks out weak government officials to bribe or bully and no one is stopping him – certainly not Reed or any of the district supervisors. If anything, they turn a blind eye. He needs to be stopped."

Finally, Rager came to his main point. "How can I do my job with all the corruption in the district office? And now an Indian chief has been beaten by two district officials and the police do nothing to investigate. If we don't do something, if we sit back and let it pass, we're as guilty as all of them put together. We might as well take up guns and begin shooting Indians – at least it would be quicker. What we're doing now is worse than murder: it's betrayal."

Stephen Majors had done his best to avoid controversy all his life. Suddenly, someone he had hired was shining a spotlight on the agency. He was shaken and spoke cautiously. Who knew what the man in front of him might do? "You know that these are very serious accusations, so let's be very careful with what we say. Let's not rock the boat without any proof, not now, not just yet." He wished he could make it all go away – what Rager described reminded him of a third world country.

"I don't know what you mean," Rager replied.

"I mean, I don't think we need to say anything right now, do we? Besides, Reed is here in another cubicle. After speaking with you on the phone, I asked him to come down. I thought it best that we hear his side of the story. He's waiting over there if we need to speak with him."

This came as a complete surprise to Rager, who had no knowledge that four days earlier the regional superintendent had phoned Mr. Reed and asked him to come to Toronto. Rager hadn't noticed the district manager's absence – and why would he, with Mr. Reed so often out of the office? Therefore, he had no knowledge that everything he reported had already been discussed between the two men, and certainly no inkling that everything was about to be buried. It would only come to him much later, in pieces. He was like a man waking up from a life of delusion.

"You've already spoken with Reed?" he asked.

"Yes, but not in any detail."

"And what did he say?"

"Reed said that you're exaggerating and out of control. He thinks you've gone a little bit cuckoo."

Rager's stomach curled. He expected that at any moment, an Ontario Provincial Police officer might suddenly appear and lead him away.

"I'm not exaggerating," he said.

"Reed says that a lot of what you say is exaggerated and that bribes were never paid. Oh, true enough, maybe someone offered someone a bribe. These things do happen; people get greedy. But money never did change hands."

At this point, Stephen appeared sad and disappointed. Here was a man he had hired who was capable of turning on the agency, a man who could exaggerate and even fabricate a story for ulterior motives. He choose, therefore, to speak carefully, measuring his words as though in a court of law explaining to a judge and jury the seriousness of the case, and how events could easily be misinterpreted. "You and I both know that there is no proof of anyone taking bribes. As for two district officials beating up an Indian chief in the middle of the night – in a dark alley, no less – well, that too seems a bit hard to swallow. Do you think if the OPP had any evidence they wouldn't investigate, lay charges, and make an arrest?"

Like any good lawyer, he answered his own question, casting doubt on the accuser. "Why, of course they would. After all, it's their job to investigate; they are the police. You only have one thing you can prove, and I believe that is the real issue underlying your complaint about Reed: the lack of action on what you refer to as the Windsor House report, which no one has seen or heard about. Is that what's really bothering you, John? Be honest with me. Are you angry that Reed has done nothing with your report?" He arched an eyebrow – a gift from his father.

"Am I correct to think that you think I'm making it all up – is that what you think of me, Stephen?" Rager replied.

"I think you're jumping to conclusions, John. A chief shows up in your office, badly beaten, tells you the police arrested the wrong man, and accuses two of your co-workers of beating him up. He may very well be looking at some form of retribution for those two men – what for, I have no idea. He could easily have been beaten by someone else; don't you think it rather convenient for an Indian chief who hates the Department of Indian Affairs to blame two agency officials? As for the bribes, perhaps your Mr. Mensen is trying to see what he can get out of you. As for buying the camps, well the man may have a point.

We never have been able to make the camps profitable. But you have absolutely no proof that others in the district office are taking bribes. No, you have none whatsoever."

"Really? You believe that all I just told you is made up?"

"Yes, I think so. But then, you look a bit under the weather, a bit tired and irritable. I wonder why?"

Rager had not slept well and it showed on his face; he was pale, more so than usual, and visibly nervous. Stephen arched his eyebrow a bit higher. It was too much for Rager to bare. He could hardly stomach the lack of concern and accountability within Indian Affairs. At all levels – district, regional, and likely Ottawa – the inaction had consequences reaching down to the Indian villages that were mired in poverty. He suddenly felt isolated in an organization where corruption, ineptitude, and violence were evident to even a fool – and now the man who had hired him was accusing him of making it all up. Rager stared at the man's cold, unflappable face. He was a younger version of Mr. Reed, a different fish in a dead sea. "I want to see David Stewart. I want to see him now!"

"I think you might regret your decision."

"I'll be the judge of that, thank you."

The regional superintendent stood and walked over to see Stewart. David Stewart's office was tastefully decorated with a Persian carpet, woodland prints and carvings, and modern Danish furniture. The man who sat at the desk was short, thin, and casually dressed in a shirt, silk tie, cashmere sweater, and Italian loafers that he could easily slip on and off as he moved about the office or sat in a leather reclining chair, crossing his legs like a well-tailored Buddha. On the wall behind his desk were a number of university degrees, with the last an LLD from Oxford. Everything about his appearance – the pointed aquiline nose, horn-rimmed glasses, the way he moved about quietly like a Siamese cat – signaled that he was someone with taste, intelligence, and an even temper.

David Stewart was a professor in the Department of Political Science at Carleton University in Ottawa, an academic with a focus on public policy who had taken a two-year leave of absence to assist the agency to draft and implement a new organizational and delivery structure in the Province of Ontario. If successful, his efforts would be duplicated throughout the country. His time with the agency also provided him an opportunity to write another book to add to the five he had already written.

When Stephen arrived in his office, he was in the middle of reading a thick government draft report. As was his habit, he used a yellow marker to highlight passages, often writing comments with a Montblanc pen and choosing his words carefully – "wood," "very good," "what do you mean?" "well said," "please! enough…enough!" "more…give me more," "please explain," "stop repeating yourself!" It was almost as though he were grading a graduate student's thesis; perhaps a student with promise but not quite up to his own high standards. He was lost in this activity when Stephen appeared. "David, he's here."

"Who?"

"John Rager, the commerce officer from Grayson."

"Oh – him. Have I ever met the man?"

"No, you haven't. But he's the one making all the noise about Reed. I'm not surprised. Reed is one of our worst district managers. Thank God he retires in January!"

Stephen repeated Rager's list of accusations, making certain to emphasize that none were proven. "It's all hearsay, one man's word against another. Once Gordon Hughes takes over, I feel confident we won't have any more of these sorts of accusations. The man's more reliable and a lot tougher. If there are bribes, they won't continue. As you know, he worked for the Hudson's Bay."

"The Bay is a good company," Stephen commented.

"One of the best – over three hundred years of history in Canada – although, as you well know, the man is poorly educated and rather crude. In my opinion, he yells too much and tries to bully. But you know that already. Nonetheless, he won't be district manager for very long – at best, six months. Once we get the Thunder Bay super district operating, a number of these district offices will be closed permanently. They do a terrible job and cost the government a great deal. There's simply too much unnecessary duplication. If we do this properly, and I know we can, we can reduce the number of staff considerably. But then, that's why I'm here, to offer solutions." The regional director general was a man with a mission.

"Of course...Reed is also here in case you need him. I've placed him in one of the empty cubicles. If need be, you can bring him in to speak, or you might not want to; it's up to you."

"I don't think I'll need to, but it's good to know. These people who work in the districts are unpredictable;

too many seem to be outright liars, drunks, thieves, or morons. I wouldn't be surprised if one or two were child molesters. The sooner we reduce their number and turn more responsibility over to the Indian bands, the better off we'll all be. The district offices should have been closed a long time ago."

"Agreed."

"Thank you."

The professor trusted no one. Everything was a matter of having a long-term vision with goals and objectives, and the organizational structure to reach those goals and objectives. Who should set the goals and objectives? The professor thought it was up to the government.

"Well, send in Mr. Rager," he said.

Rager appeared in a badly wrinkled and worn-out suit, his hair hanging down over his ears. He began to speak. "Sir..."

"Call me David."

"David, we have a problem..."

And so, he repeated all of what he had said to the regional superintendent. The professor listened without interrupting, often nodding his head in approval or squinting his eyes painfully. The professor never liked to be rushed; he preferred careful and thoughtful deliberation before acting. As he listened, he thought, "He seems like a drinker." He wished he could say to Rager, "Goodbye, have a pleasant day. Come again, my office is always open."

When it came to the Windsor House report, Stewart said, "Yes, I did receive a disturbing letter from a Sister

Brunelle, and I did phone and speak with Reed. I told him that I wouldn't tolerate leaving a village to suffer with drinking and violence to the point that it had the worst record of violence on a per capita basis in the province of Ontario. Nor would I tolerate anyone taking bribes or a school being closed for a year. I told him to address those issues and to get back to me as soon as possible. He said he would. I assume he sent you to Windsor House to follow up?"

"He did. I wrote a report in September and submitted it to Mr. Reed in October. The report essentially outlines five measures that we as an agency can take to address the needs of Windsor House. I might add, it responds to what the chief and council told me they need."

"I see – that's all very well, but I never did receive a report."

"That's because Reed never sent it to you, David,"

"That is serious. I don't like it when officials don't do what they're told to do, and that includes any of the district managers." The regional director general/professor was equally assertive about the problem of bribes and the apparent beating of a village chief. "If what you tell me is half true, it is frankly disgraceful. We can't – we won't – have any cover up. It makes us all look bad."

The term "cover up" brought into play the image of the disgraced American president who had recently been forced to resign from office. In Canada there could never be any such thing; only Americans had presidents who authorized break-ins and cover-ups and were forced to resign. Canadians had great prime ministers – statesman, moral leaders, and one of them, Prime Minister Pearson, the recipient of a Nobel Peace Prize for bringing a U.N peace force to the Middle East. Only occasionally did Canada have a vain, arrogant, ignorant prime minister.

"What do you say I have someone follow up on what you've told me? For lack of a better term, let's call him 'the inspector'; he would be someone impartial who Ottawa appoints to look into the bribes, the beating of an Indian chief, and a review of your report. Let him talk to you and everyone else involved. Let him look into all the relevant files, contracts, and basically do whatever he wants. He would gather all the relevant facts, sort out everything, and draw his own conclusions. I think this should be someone experienced with a good reputation for independent and sober thinking. What do you say?" The professor sat curled in his leather chair, cross-legged, serene, and smiled graciously. *You can trust me*, his posture seemed to say.

"I suppose it would be best," Rager agreed. "After all, how can any of us continue to work in the district if we don't take action? We need to clean up the mess and own up to what has happened."

"I couldn't agree more."

"When will the inspector be appointed?"

"Soon. Leave it with me. I know people in Ottawa who can find the right sort of person.

Believe me, I don't intend to sweep this under the rug. I am not Bob Reed."

And that was the end of Rager's two brief meetings in regional office. Mr. Reed never did attend either of the meetings. Instead, he sat alone in a cubicle, reading a travel magazine. He wondered what he would say, but he was never asked to speak. He left as soon as he could, thinking of the long drive back to Grayson, the terrible café food, the dangerous transports with drivers on drugs, and his only stop to see his cousin in Sault Ste. Marie. "I should never have come," Mr. Reed thought. "The trip was a complete waste of time, but it's the last time I'll ever have to drive to regional office. The whole thing will soon be over."

(2)

It was late in the evening when Rager left the Holiday Inn and began walking down Yonge Street. The heavy traffic, police cruisers with sirens blaring and lights flashing, and strip joints and peep shows, all the elements of a strange carnival, with the street covered in posters of semi-nude women instead of elephants, acrobats, and the man on the flying trapeze – "He'd fly through the air with the greatest of ease, a daring young man on the flying Trapeze..." – were all too prevalent.

Rager passed by the Brass Rail and Eaton's. On the spur of the moment, he purchased a coffee in a café – "Make it to go, please."

"Sure, Mister."

"Thank you."

He was a lonely, quiet man, easily lost in a downtown evening crowd; not counted, not measured, not anything. Even when he was a ten-year-old boy in the east end of Montreal, he hardly mattered to anyone except his mother.

He continued walking until he reached an eight-story apartment building on Sherbourne Street. He took the elevator to the fourth floor and got off. The hallway was extremely narrow, with the walls closing in so that each tenant could smell the others' cooking and almost reach across into a neighbor's apartment – "I need a beer." That was the feeling as he walked along the narrow corridor, as though he were returning to an all too familiar place – "Please, mister, be kind to my mother, don't hurt her. She doesn't know what she's doing."

The frail, elderly woman who opened the door was thin as a rail. At eighty-two, her osteoporosis had turned her bones into balsa wood and the stomach cancer was slowly eating her away. She had a wry smile and spoke softly. Seeing her, Rager remembered the poverty, the schools, her different boyfriends, and the times she would say, "John, don't worry, we'll figure it out. I want you to succeed, that's all that's important, nothing else, so don't worry about me. You worry about yourself."

She wrapped her arms around him and kissed him. "I love you, son, even if you work for the government." They both laughed. He could smell the gin on her breath. It was as much a part of his mother as her attempt at wearing lipstick to appear younger; an aging woman attempting not to disappoint.

"I love you, Mum," he replied.

They sat together on a sofa where the seat was falling through and the smell of food lingered like the dead smell from an alley. He listened to his mother complain about her neighbors: the awful man down the hall who watched her coming and going – "I think he steals"; the building superintendent who collected the monthly rent – "I think he expects me to give him a tip"; the large number of students who lived together – "I suppose they need to save money"; the woman who came and went with different men at all hours of the night – "I don't judge people. She needs to do what she can to survive." It was all part of the world his mother inhabited.

She told him she missed Montreal, the downtown and old Montreal – "The Nelson Hotel was where we stayed together the last night before your father left for the war. We drank far too much. He locked himself out of the room with no clothes on and had to walk down to the front desk to get a room key!" She talked of her first employer: "He was a Jewish man who owned a garment manufacturing business, and he would always walk me to the streetcar late at night after we closed the office. I know he was sweet on me." She talked about the different Montreal apartments they occupied, including the one in the basement of a house. Now she lived in the city of her youth. "I grew up in Cabbagetown, but it seems like only yesterday."

Rager listened carefully to everything she said. He told her not to worry about what the doctors had told her – "You never know, Mother, it might get better. Cancer can be beaten; try and think of the positive, always think of the positive, it's all we have in life, nothing else." He did this every night while he stayed in Toronto. When he was away, he would phone her once a week as he always did, a dutiful son, living in a rooming house in a remote town, a place she could only imagine.

"Are you happy, John, are you really and truly happy, son?"

"Yes, Mother, I am happy. I miss Sam, but you know that."

"Yes, I do. Now, you too have to be positive. You have to. You'll find someone else. I know you will. Always have hope. Never give in. Life is full of surprises. Keep up your spirits and don't let those people in government pull you down. Don't let them win – you're better than that."

"I try."

"Good."

They drank together, talked, and then he left.

Chapter 4
THE KINGDOM

The Indian Affairs and Northern Development Deputy Minister was far from being a career bureaucrat. Hugh Connors was a successful Calgary lawyer who had taken the position to help out a friend in the federal cabinet and had no intention of staying as deputy minister for any length of time, especially after working in the department for over a year and accomplishing very little. This afternoon he walked along the path beside the Rideau Canal, determined to finally resign. The agency was riddled with so many fools and incompetents that it was impossible to make any positive changes. He felt increasingly like Sisyphus pushing a boulder up a hill only to see it roll down again, or the little Dutch boy trying to keep the dam from bursting by placing his finger in one hole only to see another spring to life, or the man who had fallen into a trap set by those long before him and was doomed to failure, while the senior bureaucrats in their rich leather coats cared not a thing whether he stayed or left. "Why did I ever take this position? I must have been an idiot," he thought.

The man who walked beside him, François Gravelle, was the Assistant Deputy Minister, a seasoned bureaucrat and a very different animal. He knew every nook and cranny in the capital city, and every deep buried secret. He was cheery, friendly, fluently bilingual, and could easily have been a diplomat. He lived not far from Ottawa in the Gatineau Hills, while Hugh lived in a two-bedroom apartment off Wellington Street.

Hugh always enjoyed the afternoon walks, a practice he had started one day and now felt obliged to continue. He had good reasons to walk, what with the meetings between and within departments, conference calls across the country, a parade of lawyers and policy people waiting to brief him on this or that subject, memos and letters to write, new policies to consider, Treasury Board submissions to submit and defend, fights with other departments for increased funding, who to hire, who to let go, who to contract, who to brief, who to say yes and no to, and so on, and none of it reaching very far to make a real difference in the lives of Indigenous people or, for that matter, to stem his high blood pressure – not even the new pills his doctor had prescribed did much; he still suffered terrible headaches. So, the walks helped. They were a way of letting off steam and soothing a troubled legal mind more accustomed to working for big oil companies – where timely results meant something – and not the slow, painful pace of bureaucratic work in a mean city that pretended it was so much more. The dirty underwear of Ottawa would have killed a city of roaches.

It was near Christmas and the ice on the Rideau Canal had formed. Passersby stopped to watch a couple skating as though they were trained professionals in the Ice Capades. People were bundled tightly in winter coats, tuques, scarves, and boots, even the odd beaver hat, or a wool knitted hat from the Northwest Territories. Christmas carols blared from outdoor speakers, men dressed like Santa Clause stood beside Salvation Army kettles ringing bells, and the CBC reporters stood outside the parliament buildings waiting to interview politicians. No one paid much attention to the homeless crowding the tunnel across from the Chateau Laurier, the prostitutes in the Market area, and least of all to two government officials walking beside the Rideau Canal and sipping coffee.

The two men took their time. They walked slowly and talked quietly, each man listening to the other and each sipping a coffee laced with sugar and cream. Before leaving headquarters on Laurier. Hugh had said, "The office is a trap, François. I can't get anything done without being interrupted. I have no time to think." It was the reason they had left the office and driven over to the new head-quarters in the Terrasses de la Chaudière under construction. "Let's go," Hugh had said; François followed him out the door, down the stairs, into the parking lot, and into Hugh's new Volvo. Hugh drove the short distance over the bridge to Hull, where they parked and inspected the building. Both men asked the construction supervisor a few questions. François knew Robert Campeau, the developer, and felt it important to let the supervisor know that he was well connected. They drove back, parked the car, bought coffee, and began to walk. It would soon be five o'clock and the office on Laurier would be empty – except for Hugh, François, and a half-dozen staff who would stay behind and work long into the evening making phone calls. Hugh might run off to brief the minister – a former insurance broker – who seemed more interested in drinking and chasing women than introducing new policies.

François was a dark, handsome, highly educated government official; a French-Canadian with no hint of an accent and no need to apologize to anyone for using either of the official languages poorly. He was a man who believed strongly in the policy of a bilingual civil service and had for as long as the policy existed. Prime Minister Trudeau was a great force for change in Canada, and Quebec could do no better than to have one of its own in charge. François was also a wine expert, an oenologist, who could speak knowledgeably on the soil and grapes of the great vineyards in France, Italy, Spain, Portugal, and more recently, California. In the dark, cool basement of his home in the Gatineau Hills, he stored a thousand bottles of wine.

He had also recently developed a new hobby of riding horses – something his new girlfriend, a researcher in the department, had introduced him to. "If I had known before the freedom of riding a horse, the joy that a horse can give, I would have taken up riding a long time ago," he thought. His wife, a cardiologist, had no interest in horses, although she enjoyed a glass or two of wine, as did his children, one at Princeton studying medicine and another in Paris studying philosophy. He would see them both at Christmas.

Hugh had no interest in wines or horses or girlfriends. He was a hard-nosed Calgary lawyer with a background in negotiating land claims and resource development agreements. He had worked with Indians in Alberta, Saskatchewan, and more recently, the Inuvialuit in the Northwest Territories. It was for this reason that his cabinet friend had asked him to take the position of deputy minister. "I'll give you one year to get the department into shape and then I'm gone," Hugh had said. But now it seemed that a year was not long enough.

When he first started, a senior Treasury Board official had told Hugh what to expect: "The department is riddled with dead weight, fools, and people who can barely tie their own shoelaces. The minister can never stay away from a bottle or a woman – on trips across the country, he offers himself shamelessly to women in bars, conferences, meetings, even on elevators. He's an embarrassment to the government, but there you have it. The department is cursed and there's no way to change anything except to tear it down. I'm telling you this so hopefully you can bring in new people. God knows the Indians need it."

They had just finished a long discussion on the need for a new Indian and Inuit employment and training program and the difficulty in obtaining Department of Manpower approval for the program. They had also discussed a rumour that a woman had complained to the police about the minister trying to assault her when François mentioned that he had received a memo from the Ontario regional director general. "I received a memo from Stewart yesterday asking for an investigation into the

Nakina district. As you know, it's going to be amalgamated into one of our super districts. It appears that two district officials may have been involved in beating up an Indian chief – no proof, mind you, but still very serious. There are also concerns that one of the officials has been taking bribes from an air charter company. Moreover, a Catholic nun recently wrote a letter to Stewart making all sorts of accusations. He wants us to appoint an inspector to look into the matter."

"François, this is precisely the sort of stuff that brought me out here."

François nodded his head. "Yes, I know, Hugh. If it is true, it is very serious. If the media gets wind of this, it could hurt the department terribly."

"What does Stewart want us to do?"

"He recommends we send someone with audit experience to look into all the issues, then write a report letting us know what he discovered and what we should do. I know it draws things out, but maybe that's what we need. An experienced professional with a fresh set of eyes."

"What about the police – shouldn't they be involved in determining if district officials beat up an Indian chief? I mean, if this was Alberta, I can tell you that the police would be doing their job. I don't think the Bloods or Blackfeet would take this lightly."

"The chief is Ojibwa, from a remote village named Otter Falls. I wouldn't worry about any protest. I also think we have to keep this in perspective. There is no proof that the officials in question did anything wrong, so we have to be discreet. We don't want this thing blown up out of all proposition or, God forbid, getting out to the media. If it ever got out that two Indian Affairs officials beat up a chief, you can just imagine what it would to the department's reputation. The issue of bribes is another matter, and we can easily handle that sort of thing."

"So, we look for an auditor?"

"At this point, yes. After all, it's not a criminal matter, at least not yet – and I don't think we want to raise it to that level, at least not now, and hopefully never. If they are guilty of taking bribes, we can arrange for their transfer to another district, or buy them out, which is often the best option. We have enough issues without adding more to our plate."

There were many issues on their plate that day. There was a growing anger across the country among different Indigenous groups demanding greater control over the delivery of government programs and services, a greater share in the wealth and prosperity of the nation, and a greater respect for the intent of the Treaties – not what was written, but what was understood to be a relationship between two sovereign peoples. There was a growing concern over the American Indian Movement entering into Canada with their militant approach to politics. Only a few years before, AIM had become deeply involved in the armed occupation of Wounded Knee on the Pine Ridge Indian Reservation, and there was a deep concern that Indigenous groups in Canada might follow their example. There was the reality that Indigenous people in Canada suffered disproportionately with poverty, unemployment, crowded housing, broken families, high suicide rates, and higher incarceration rates in the federal and provincial prisons, a misery that affected their communities and families from coast to coast to coast. Then there were pending land claim agreements that needed to be settled. Hugh always felt that it was a great shame that land claims had not been settled, but that was the reality, the plain truth, and he understood more than anyone that the political will to enter into new land claims was simply not a high priority with the public – and therefore the politicians.

There were the different federal departments and agencies that never seemed to be able to work together on delivering programs or services. Funding was tight, what with federal government priorities shifting from one thing to another like a man twirling a Rolodex and the provinces refusing to provide funding because of the constitutional separation of powers. There was the Berger Inquiry, which had yet to make its final recommendations on the Mackenzie Valley pipeline – and oil money was very much at stake. The pipeline was one of the reasons they had brought in Hugh to shake things up, to stimulate northern development, what with his contacts with the Dene and the Inuvialuit. But here he was, worrying about a minister assaulting a woman and two officials in a remote district he knew nothing about taking bribes and beating up an Indian chief. What else was there? If he walked around headquarters, Hugh would often see staff reading newspapers, or dead asleep at their desks, or simply gone – he had once seen a program manager sneaking into a peep show in Hull in the early afternoon. It was worse than herding cats. As he thought of all that was on his plate, he began to have a bad headache. "François, take care of it, please. I don't want to hear anymore!"

They continued their walk, neither man wanting to get back to the office. They spoke about a conference call scheduled for later that evening. It didn't matter who the participants were or the topic of discussion; it was just one more among an endless number of conference calls, meetings, unscheduled trips, special inquiries, task forces, a great parade of government officials meeting with Indian leaders, and more often than not, the senior officials deciding what or what not to do, and then revising budgets, re-scheduling decisions, rescheduling meetings, trying this and that, and approving funding – never quite enough – or delaying. It would continue for decades. Even though the players' faces changed, the same song continued: make promises, do as little as possible, just talk and talk and talk until everyone gives up and walks away.

Chapter 5:
THE INSPECTOR

(1)

At one time, Tom Blackwell had been an important Treasury Board official, a policy wonk who once wrote a report on benefit-cost analysis that was so succinct and well written, it was printed and circulated throughout the higher echelons of the federal government. But after having an affair with a young secretary half his age, yelling and berating staff, questioning his superiors, and having his wife and children leave him, he had fallen on hard times. It seemed that Tom had too high an opinion of himself, shown first in his belief that he was something of a genius, and then by succumbing to a young secretary's charms and flattery. It wasn't long before he began drinking alone in the middle of the day, meeting prostitutes, and buying and selling stocks until he was bankrupt.

Nothing was ever done to counsel Tom – not even after the security guards found him in the office one night, naked and having sex with a woman. It wasn't until he broke down in a meeting and began sobbing – "I don't know what's happening to me. I don't know. I need help!" – that he was taken away and diagnosed as bipolar. Tom was eventually taken to the Royal Ottawa Hospital (ROH), where he was treated and stayed for three months. When released, he was overweight and heavily medicated. At that point, Treasury Board decided it was best for everyone if he went on permanent disability. Tom moved into a rooming house and began to read books on religion, hopeful that one day he might return to Treasury Board, where he would write another paper on benefit-cost analysis.

It was through an old friend within the Treasury Board that Indian Affairs contracted Tom to be the inspector and sent him to Grayson.

The inspector arrived in Grayson in mid-January 1977, confident that he was more than able to meet his contract obligations. He began by interviewing Rager and Gordon Hughes. Then he moved on to Freddy Birch, Olaf Jehkinen, the police staff sergeant, and the bartender at the Main Hotel. All interviews were written on yellow foolscap paper and later typed up so they were clear and legible. While in Grayson, he collected what information he could – copies of contracts, memos between officials, Sister Brunelle's letter, and Rager's Windsor House report. He followed this up by driving to Nakina to interview Teddy Mensen, then flew north to Otter Falls to interview Elijah Wappose. Finally, he drove to Thunder Bay to interview Mr. Reed before returning to Ottawa. Tom kept all the collected information in two four-inch, three-hole binders with tabs carefully labelled for different sections – interviews, contracts, reports, and so forth. These two binders contained all the information he needed to write his report, which he submitted in mid-February 1977.

It was somewhat strange to hear later that Tom attended a Rotary Club luncheon during his time in Grayson, where he introduced himself as a retired Treasury Board director general doing consulting work for Indian Affairs. It was during the luncheon that he spoke at length about the lack of the "right sort" of people working in government – specifically those with experience in benefit-cost analysis. By that, he meant people who could analyze government expenditures according to "inputs" – not only the amount of funding allocated for programs and services, but also how a department was staffed and organized (in the case of Indians Affairs, a number of small district offices) – against "outputs" – for the Indian villages, these included employment and income, better living conditions, and less dependence on government.

In Tom's opinion, Indian Affairs was spending far too much time on inputs and not enough on measuring outputs. "If you think about it, the department spends too much time focusing on the size of its own bureaucracy and whether they should have small district offices or super districts, instead of demonstrating what the Indians obtain for what the department does. Unfortunately, they simply do not know whether they are getting 'bang for buck.' There is zero accountability, not only to the Indians they are mandated to serve, but ultimately the taxpayer, you and I. In short, they need to change the way they operate. In fact, they need to change their culture, putting the Indians first, listening to what they need, and not themselves. They need to make sure that the money they do spend does the most good, not the size of the bureaucracy."

Tom gave a number of examples of where the department might achieve better results if they focused on outputs. If Indian families were housed in safer, warmer houses, their children would arrive in school well-rested, families would have longer and more fruitful lives, and government would achieve lower long-term health care costs. Companies supplying villages with housing materials and the airlines shipping materials would benefit from increased spending. If the government invested more in education, training, and economic development, it would reduce social assistance and lead to more independent self-reliant Indian communities. Over time the savings would be considerable.

"Think of Indians with their own airlines, mining exploration companies, sawmills, and tourist lodges. Why, they could be some of the largest operators in northwestern Ontario. Instead of having to rely on welfare, they would contribute to the regional economy. How can the agency achieve those results? One way would be to turn over the funding and delivery of programs and services to the Indians themselves and support new and innovative approaches, focusing on results."

Then Tom turned his attention to the provincial government, saying it was high time that the province took on more responsibility. "The provinces should provide more support for Indian villages, for example, by placing permanent police officers in the villages and building roads and airports – forget constitutional haggling. Who cares where the money comes from? It has to be done. It only hurts the people who live in the villages. Honestly, as a Canadian I think it's something we can't afford to continue. I suppose it comes down to political leadership and accountable government agencies." Then he took a swipe at his former employer, who had left him out in the cold. "If you ask any manager within a federal department what they see as priorities, they tell you they need more staff. The reality is that they need fewer staff; the savings could be allocated to where it's most needed. We don't need more government officials, we need fewer. The saying 'less is more' certainly applies to the federal government."

Finally, Tom spoke about economic development as a cornerstone to any new Indian Affairs initiative. "In my opinion, the department spends far too little on economic development to have any real impact on the lives of Indians. All they do is spend the least amount to keep Indians dependent on government. They may think it's well meaning, but in the long term it is destructive."

Everyone attending the meeting was impressed. The mayor spoke for everyone when he said, "Sir, we need more people like you in government. I am sorry to hear that you're retired. At least the federal government has shown the good sense to keep you on contract. In my humble opinion, they should give you a medal!" Tom received a standing ovation.

(2)

Tom Blackwell's visit did very little to help Rager. If anything, the inspector's visit proved to be destructive. Those who worked in the district office were suddenly cold and distant. Whenever he arrived back from a trip, no one bothered to ask, "How was your trip?" or give any indication he was ever missed. Gordon Hughes, the new district manager, even went so far as to tell the other officers that Rager was finished with Indian Affairs – "He lives in a rooming house, doesn't tell anyone what he's doing and drinks too much. He's a loner and certainly not the type we need in the agency."

But this was false. Rager had cut back on his drinking considerably and continued to work with Indians to start businesses, often writing business plans and funding proposals. He even went out of his way to help the happy-go-lucky supervisor of social services launch a number of innovative make-work projects. On top of that, he was involved with the agency-owned tourist camps: he attended sportfishing trade shows in Minneapolis and Toronto, consulted with tourism wholesalers, enlisted the support of sportfishing magazine writers to promote the camps, and continued to work on establishing a fly-in Indian village-owned development corporation to own and operate the camps. Indeed, Rager worked harder than anyone else in the district office, staying late at night and usually over the weekends. But it didn't matter much. Most everyone in the district office was out to destroy the "whistleblower." That was how they saw him: a traitor who had turned on his colleagues.

In all of this, no one ever mentioned that the underlying reason for their hostility was that his accusation of taking bribes was against everyone, from the lowest paid clerk-secretary who typed up contracts and witnessed signatures to Mr. Reed and the district supervisors who turned a blind eye. As for Elijah, he was no friend of the Ontario Provincial Police sergeant, a well-respected local policeman who pointed out that no decent OPP constable under *his* command would ever condone two government officials beating up an Indian chief without lifting a finger. The accusations were just too much for anyone in Grayson to take seriously.

There were those, too, in regional office – especially Stephen – who felt betrayed by the man he had hired. As a consequence, Stephen began sending memos requesting more detail on Rager's work and travel plans and followed these up with phone calls – "From now on, I need to know everything you're doing or planning to do. No more travelling without my prior approval. Do you understand?" There was also more scrutiny of Rager's funding applications on behalf of Indian applicants; every submission was checked and double checked, every word was looked over, every figure scrutinized, and questions were asked that were none too complimentary – "Where did you get your market information? How did you calculate the return on investment? Please use the following business ratios and provide more detail." The secretary to the Indian Small Business Loan Fund even went so far as to ask, "Do you know what you're doing?"

The change in attitude made Rager's work more difficult – almost impossible – and eventually he knew it was only a matter of time before they found a reason to terminate his employment. He could already imagine Stephen's performance appraisal in April. "John Rager works alone and does not collaborate with colleagues. His applications for funding on behalf of clients are generally poor and rejected. His performance for the year has been far from satisfactory." He could appeal the appraisal, but to who, and to what end? The agency officials were closing ranks, shutting doors, and in the process teaching him a good lesson: "Turn on one of us and you'll be gone."

Where was the evidence to support Rager's accusations? Tom Blackwell had found none. Mr. Reed was no fool on matters that concerned his welfare. He ensured that district files concerning Mensen beyond twelve months were burned in the town dump, while more recent files showed that good service was the overriding factor in awarding contracts. What did "good service" mean? According to those interviewed by Tom, it was a complex and subjective factor that meant at least two things: 1) providing service on short notice, and 2) providing the type of preferred aircraft. The inspector accepted that good service was, therefore, a difficult factor to measure. More comment should have been provided to bidders, but under the circumstances, officials could be excused. After all, as he wrote, "The officials are the ones who define good service, and no one else. More importantly, there is no evidence of anyone receiving bribes." There was only hearsay, one person's word against another. In this case, it was Rager's word against everyone else.

On the second issue – Freddy and Olaf beating up the chief of Otter Falls – again there was no evidence. However, there *was* ample evidence that Elijah was a heavy drinker and a troublemaker. According to the police sergeant, whenever Elijah came to town, he would get drunk in a hotel or hole up in a room and start drinking, sometimes not even bothering to come out of his room.

"I know one time we were called to break down the door to get to him," the sergeant said. "When we did, the room was a mess: furniture broken apart, television broken, and the sheets soiled where he crapped his pants. He was barely breathing and it was lucky we got him to a hospital." Elijah was known to get into fights. "Just ask the hotel managers and they'll tell you he gets into fights too easily and is all around bad news. I wouldn't trust anything he says."

Sure enough, Elijah's name was anathema to the hotel managers, who said that renting him a room was asking for trouble. "You never know if he's going to get drunk and break up the furniture," they said. "He lies, too – tells you that other people are responsible." It appeared the beating was just another example of his invented stories. Freddy and Olaf had nothing to do with the incident. More to the point, Rager was a poor judge of character, accusing two decent, hard-working colleagues of beating someone up based solely on the words of the accuser, namely Elijah.

"Seems to me he's an Indian-lover," one of the managers said.

The only remaining issue was the Windsor House report, of which Tom Blackwell had been given a copy to read and felt obliged to provide comment – in doing so, the inspector took his time in writing what he believed to be the unadulterated truth.

Rager was a "man of conscience," Tom wrote. By that he meant a man who believed that too many Indians had suffered injustice under federal government policies and more should be done to improve their quality of life, including providing an increased investment in economic development. This was a cause Tom Blackwell supported, but it was one that required deeper analysis. How was this to be accomplished? According to the inspector, it required increased spending and benefit-cost analysis. Here he took his time in explaining what he meant. He started with one example, the reopening and subsidizing of the Windsor House sawmill. It could have been the tourist camps, houses, recreation hall, school, piped water, sewage service, or a water treatment plant – in fact, anything and everything including relocating the village – but he selected the portable sawmill to demonstrate how everything in the Windsor House report could be analyzed. He did this in point form:

1. **Issue Definition:** The sawmill was closed because there was no government subsidy. Assuming there was a market for lumber (e.g., repairing houses and building new houses), should the sawmill be re-opened?
2. **Baseline Scenario:** The cost of not subsidizing the sawmill was defined as the baseline scenario. Given enough time, the sawmill would fall into complete disrepair and no longer be salvageable.
3. **Alternatives:** Low investment (if needed, repair the equipment); medium investment (purchase new equipment); and high investment (build a new building and purchase new equipment).

4. **Costs:** Tom outlined the capital and operating costs for each scenario.

5. **Benefits:** The full range of benefits included: seasonal employment and income for those harvesting timber and working in the sawmill; repaired houses; more tourist camps; an opportunity to relocate the sawmill to a new village should the government decide to build a new village; the multiplier effect from money spent at the Hudson Bay store; and savings from using local timber versus more expensive imported lumber.

6. **Sensitivity Analysis:** Tom provided tables to show the impact of different levels of investment.

Tom recommended that the agency undertake this sort of analysis on all the report-recommended priorities. It all depended on your assumptions, he wrote, whether or not you thought the government should invest in improving the quality of life of those living in Windsor House. He left it to more senior officials to decide.

After he read Tom Blackwell's report, David Stewart decided there was no basis to Rager's accusations. As for the Windsor House report, he assigned a junior officer to undertake more research and analysis. In reality, this meant the report would be shelved and no further action taken. In the interim, Rager was left out in the cold; Tom had not sought his input, other than interviewing him on the beating of Elijah and the bribes, nor did he share his report with him. He was left with Gordon standing over his shoulder until April, when Stephen would undertake his performance appraisal, knowing he would be forced to resign.

Gordon left little doubt as to Rager's future when he told him, "You know that Blackwell's report found no truth to your claims about bribes and Freddy and Olaf beating up Elijah. As for your Windsor House report, Stewart has given it to someone to do more research and analysis. My own point of view is that it's a terrible plan. My God, can you imagine if all the villages started asking for more funding for housing, education, and everything else, let alone to be relocated so they could have airports? It would never end – why, they might even start asking for water treatment plants. Think of the cost! Did you never think that would be a factor?"

Tom Blackwell was never brought back to Treasury Board. The following summer on a humid night, bitter, disappointed, living alone in a rooming house, and no longer wanting to take his prescribed medication, he hanged himself with a belt tied to a door.

Chapter 6
AN UNEXPECTED MEETING

When Marie Brunelle left the Sisters of Charity, an order dedicated to serving the "poorest of the poor," after eight years, she knew that she would have to find a new path. As she put it to her superior, "We as a church are as guilty as the government when it comes to what we did to those children in the residential schools. I can no longer remain part of the Church. I have to leave and find my own path." Counselling women as a lay social worker in a Toronto woman's shelter was all Marie needed to feel satisfied. She continued to attend mass and receive the sacrament; the teachings of Christ were too deep in her soul. But the Catholic church's protection of monsters was another matter.

In late-February of 1977, she was approached at the shelter by a man with deeply troubled eyes. When he spoke to her, she felt as though she were speaking with someone searching for answers.

"Sister Brunelle?" he asked.

"You mean Marie Brunelle."

"Yes, I apologize. Marie? My name is John Rager. I'm the Nakina District Indian Affairs Commerce Officer. I'm aware of the letter you sent to David Stewart last August. You should know that Mr. Reed sent me to Windsor House to see what the agency could do to remedy the problems you identified."

"You mean the problems that Indian Affairs created?"

Rager continued. "I spoke with the chief and council, Luke, Father Benoît, and a few residents. We came up with a number of recommendations to help the village. I wrote a report outlining those recommendations and submitted the report last October."

"And?"

He hesitated before answering. "I'm still waiting to hear what the agency plans to do. I expect it takes time to reach a decision, especially with Indian Affairs."

"I'm not surprised," Marie said. "Your agency is one of the worst culprits in the sad saga of Windsor House. So few in the country know the full extent of how the agency operates or, I should say, what the agency hides. Only the Indians know, and no one listens to their cries for help – least of all your agency. If you read my letter, then you know this has been going on for decades."

He winced every time she said "your agency." The idea that he belonged with Indian Affairs was as far from the truth as eternity.

"I suppose I'm one of the few who does know. However, I share your feelings – I too am disgusted."

"What can I do for you?" Marie asked.

They retreated to a coffee shop with few customers and spoke quietly for a long time. Rager told her about himself: that he was new to Indian Affairs and that he was divorced, his wife and son had left him three years earlier when they lived in Sioux Lookout, where he worked for the Ontario Cooperative Development Corporation. He told her as much as he could about the system of bribes, as well as Elijah's beating, and Tom Blackwell's report, which found no support for his accusations.

In turn, Marie told him about herself: how she grew up in Quebec, her decision to become a nun, and then leaving the order. She told him as much as she could about what she knew of the residential schools, the treatment of Indians, the failure of the church, and what the villagers in Windsor House had told her about the bribes.

They connected like two people who have waited forever to meet, as though the connection were meant to be. This strange man visiting a Toronto woman's shelter in the cold, bleak days of February found himself wondering, "Why did I track her down? What reason have I to look up the woman who started all this? But I must. I must." She listened and attempted to answer his questions because she had to, because she too felt that she must, and because she would. At one point, she said, "You play the eye game well, John."

"What do you mean?

"You hide your thoughts behind your eyes, yet you're always searching. 'Should I trust her or him?' You don't trust people, do you, John?"

"Not really. I know I have a problem."

"Why?"

He answered truthfully. "My childhood was difficult. My mother had boyfriends. They were not always nice… to either her or me." He paused, not certain of what she would say.

"I see. So, you hide your thoughts, yet you pretend to care. Even when you do care – which I believe you do – you still fail to act. It is only our actions that define us, John, not our thoughts or words. You hide, John, you hide so well. It is no wonder that your wife and son left you. It's a hard lesson to learn, but you must do better, much better. Stay strong, shoulders back, and don't wince," she said.

And he did.

But then, who was this woman to lecture him?

At one point, Rager said, "I think I can bring a lot of what I know about the bribes out into the open if…" he hesitated. "If I plan a ruse. I could convince Mensen that I'm willing to take bribes to help him secure the tourist camps, document carefully what he gives me in bribes, and send it to the police. Only then would the agency be forced to act or, at the very least, fire people. I think it might also help to open up an investigation into the people who beat up Elijah. All he was doing was telling the truth, and Freddy and Olaf took their revenge. There needs to be an accounting – there needs to be justice."

"You have to be careful," Marie said. "The man you speak about, Mensen, is a brute and a monster. One of the villagers told me that he raped a girl of fourteen and forced her into prostitution. She now lives in Winnipeg, a young woman of eighteen, a drug addict who works on the streets, a woman who will not live long. Don't you think he has done that more than once? There are other villages, other Indian girls. What else is such a man capable of doing?" She paused and took her time before speaking again. "There is something else about Mr. Mensen that you should know. When I found out about his activities in the district, I asked a member of our order in the Netherlands to research his background. She wrote me that after the war and before immigrating to Canada, he changed his name from Rotmensen to Mensen. Now I ask you, why would a man do that? Because there is evidence that he was a soldier with the Germans during the occupation – it was the Waffen-SS, a notorious branch of the Nazis. He is a dangerous man, John. Know who you are dealing with – be careful."

"That doesn't surprise me. Nothing surprises me. My superior, the Ontario Superintendent of Economic Development, will do my performance appraisal in April. I'm certain that I'll be forced to resign. I have no future with Indian Affairs – not that I want one. The agency is a terrible organization. They care nothing for Indians; they care nothing for other people except themselves,"

"I'm not surprised either," Marie said. "The agency closed the school in Windsor House instead of repairing the building. They do everything in their power so people will leave."

Rager replied, "Gordon Hughes, the current district manager, is the former district supervisor of local government. He told me once that he thought the government should close down the villages and amalgamate them into a large center to save money. It was almost as though he were talking about setting up a system of apartheid, like they have in South Africa. It made me think he and others might want to pursue that sort of strategy in other villages."

"I think that's true," Marie said. "The government always wanted to destroy the Indian culture – their 'Indianness.' The most recent example is the 1969 White Paper, which called for an end to the special relationship between the federal government and Indians and the dismantling of the Indian Act. So far, the opposition to the paper has held the government's hand, but I think the bureaucracy is another matter. Bureaucrats always hold the real power; they interpret the rules and allocate the funding. The system of bribes you describe is just one example."

"The White Paper was a terrible idea," Rager said. "It was a betrayal of the treaties and the intent of the treaties."

"Then you must act soon, before worse betrayals happen. We both know that the future for Windsor House is devastation. Indian Affairs will do as little as possible to help the villagers overcome what the government has created with the church as an ally. Guilt – there is no guilt if no one sees the sin. The public never sees the sin, and even if they do, they pretend it is the Indian's fault."

"Blame the victim," Rager said.

"Yes, blame the victim."

"Or kill the victim."

"That may be true – out of neglect."

"And keep them under control at all costs."

She nodded. "Yes. Mr. Reed does not like Windsor House, that is why he never visited the village. Of course, he seldom visited any of the district villages unless it was absolutely necessary. But with Windsor House, it was special. He detested Luke, our band administrator."

"Why?"

"Because Luke is intelligent – perhaps too intelligent. He too is an angry soul."

"Why?"

"You must ask him. You know that secrets can kill people. Everyone has secrets, John, including Mr. Reed. Even you, I would think, have secrets." She gave him a knowing look. "And I too have secrets. We all do, and that is what makes us human."

"Yes, we all have secrets." Rager felt the weight of his own secrets like a heavy stone around his neck. He gazed at Marie. She was a small, compact woman with an attractive face, her dark blue eyes full of mystery, intelligence, and kindness. "You know I am a Christian. Even after all I know about the failings of the Catholic Church, I still believe what Christ taught us. There are two commandments that you must follow: the first is, 'Thou shalt love the Lord thy God with all thy heart, and with all thy soul, and with all thy mind.' This is the first and greatest commandment. And the second is, 'Thou shalt love thy neighbour as thyself.' What do you think those two commandments mean? Let me answer for you. The first commandment is a mystery. It is, frankly, the deepest mystery. I often think of God as a mist that moves through every part of the universe, a mist that carries the very essence of life, and yet the mist does not intrude or disturb. It is love, John – God is love – and you must love God. The second commandment is an elaboration of the first. We must love one another, but it is for us to decide to love, we alone must decide. And if we love our neighbor, then we must act. Words alone mean very little." She stared at him with purpose.

"I haven't done much," he said. "I process applications, I wander around, I consult village chiefs and councils. I work with people who want to start businesses but get very little in support from the agency. I feel their pain. I do my best."

"Your best is not enough. If it was, we wouldn't be here talking. You have to act, and act soon, very soon. Never be frightened to act, but use your intelligence. Don't be a fool, above all; be wise and listen to your heart. What beats in your chest has merit. It counts, as much as what you breathe. It is one of God's gifts – among many others." Marie looked into Rager's eyes and read everything about him, as though she had known him forever.

(2)

After they talked at the café for a long time, Marie took Rager by the hand and led him away. They went to a bar, and then a second. At different times, she opened up to him and he did to her. Their conversation was that of two people trying their best to tell the other their deepest thoughts. In some ways they were trying to tell each other everything about themselves before it was too late, to say what they had to say before the final curtain came down. At one point they found themselves in a park sitting together on a bench. They were alone; it was dark and the park seemed like a church, with trees instead of an altar.

"You're always searching, John, but here is a question: what are you searching for?"

"Hope," he replied.

"Still, you have doubt. I can see it in your eyes. Doubt prevents hope. It is the work of the Devil. I am not speaking of doubt as a sense of precaution or skepticism. I am speaking of profound doubt in one's belief about themselves and who they are. You must know that the residential schools made the children doubt in everything – the love of their parents and the love of themselves. You seem to suffer from the same doubt. Why do you suffer, John? Do you not love yourself?"

"Not much," he replied. "I think it comes from my mother and the lies she told me. She said that we would have a better future, a nicer apartment, and then she brought home another boyfriend, a pretend father, a drunk…a molester." He suddenly stopped speaking and his eyes watered. "I buried everything that happened so deeply that no one would know. I felt shame…deep, deep shame."

"Did you tell your mother?"

"No."

"Your wife?"

"No."

Marie took his hand and held it. "I'm so sorry to hear that you had a difficult childhood. But we all suffer, John, some far more than others. Life is never fair – you only have to look around to see the unfairness of life. You must overcome these painful memories – most especially those memories that feed doubt about your own value. You have value, John. You are worthy of love, and you are a handsome man, perhaps a bit shy, but good to look at."

He whispered. "You don't know what it was like."

She reached over, ran her finger over his nose and cheeks, and kissed him. The softness of her kiss was like the mist of God in the universe. It seemed to free him.

"So let me tell you how to have hope. It lies in your heart, John. And what does your heart tell you?"

He replied, "That I must act to help the villages. Windsor House is the first village, the very worst, the one the agency abandoned, but there are eight others. God knows what will happen to them over time."

"Then you must act – and you must act soon. Even if you fail in finding justice for those who have been maligned, cheated, and beaten, at least you will have tried, and that is all we are asked to do: to try our best, our *very* best."

Then Marie stopped. "Enough," she said. "Let's have some fun tonight." And she kissed him.

The rest of that night, they crawled through sleezy downtown bars until they found themselves back in her apartment, on the upper floor of an older house downtown. They talked about everything. At one point, she said, "You know that one of the first things I did when I left the order was have sex with a man? He was almost a complete stranger. I suppose I needed to find my humanity, my sexuality, and I did. It was liberating. And you, why are you not with a woman?"

"I don't really know. I suppose I haven't found anyone."

"Maybe you will," she said.

"Maybe I will. Besides, I'm getting tired of living alone in a rooming house with another man."

"You need more?"

"Yes, I need more."

It was late when he left the apartment. He walked along a street full of old houses, thinking of a future and someone who could play the 'eye game' better than anyone – someone who knew him, someone he respected. He began to walk with more purpose – and more anger – as he thought of what he must do.

Part Four

Chapter 1
TAKING BRIBES

(1)

Rager never did read the inspector's report. He inquired but was told it was only for the eyes of senior officials. Instead, Stephen phoned and told him that nothing had been discovered to support his accusations. "There was not one shred of evidence to support what you said. Nothing – absolutely nothing! I think your accusations were inappropriate and completely unfair. At the very least, you should offer Freddy and Olaf an apology." Rager knew this meant that Freddy, Olaf, and Mensen would walk away scot-free. It led him to take a different direction.

On Main Street there were mountains of snow and a truck moving at a crawl. In the cold, bitter February wind, the exhaust fumes disappeared instantly. The rooming house was empty, the sole other tenant had left permanently, and the light in the hall cast a long dark shadow down the stairs to the front door. He could barely hear the steps crackling on the hard frozen ground as the man reached the front door and knocked. When Rager opened the door, a dark figure in a parka appeared. "Are you alone?" Teddy asked.

"Yes, I'm alone," he replied.

The Dutchman entered without bothering to remove his heavy winter boots. He followed Rager up to the bedroom, the snow falling off his boots to leave a trail of filthy water. He removed his parka, let it fall onto the floor, and sat down in a chair, his heavy paunch falling over his belt. Rager sat opposite. "You live alone?" Teddy asked.

"Yes, I live alone."

"No one else in the building?"

"There is no one else, the rooming house is empty. The other tenant moved out."

"Good."

A day earlier, Rager had phoned Mensen to say that he had a change of heart on the agency camps. "I don't think the Indian bands are ready to take over ownership of the camps. They have no money or business experience, so there's no good reason not to let you own them, especially if you can help renovate and modernize the camps. You also told me that you were willing to generate more employment for the villagers, so that is an important consideration, especially if I'm going to help you secure ownership and government funding. But we need to talk first. I need to know that there's something in this for me." He explained that he was under watch, had no long-term future with Indian Affairs, and had decided to accept a bribe. "We have to be careful, though. I don't want anyone to find out."

The Dutchman smiled. "Don't worry. I don't want any trouble from the government."

"Neither do I."

The Dutchman's heavy jowls along with the blond tufts of hair along his cheek and neck where he had failed to shave properly gave his face a porcine appearance. Every time he took a breath the sweat poured down his cruel face; he kept wiping it away with a filthy handkerchief. Not so long ago the Dutchman had worn a field-grey army uniform and interrogated people. It was different now. He was in a rooming house in a northern Canadian town, speaking with a younger man who was finally willing to listen to reason.

"Tell me again how we do this."

"I write a proposal that outlines how you plan to renovate and modernize the camps, then you launch an aggressive promotion and marketing campaign to draw more customers. Through synergy with your existing operation, we increase camp revenues, which results in more employment and income for the five fly-in Indian villages and, of course, more profits for your own company. You submit the proposal to regional office and wait for a response."

"What does that mean, synaa...?"

"Synergy means that the agency camps and your own camps and lodges operate under one company, namely your own company, which saves on operating costs – administration, promotion, marketing, and transportation. For example, you save with your planes servicing both the agency camps and your own camps according to the most efficient routes, giving you more opportunity for 'back-to-back flights,' the same applies to promotion and marketing. As a result, both camps benefit and generate more employment for the villages. One and one equals not two, but three – synergy."

They both knew this was a lie. When it came to the villages, Mensen would employ fewer Indians and keep all the profits. One and one, at least for the Indian villages, would equal closer to zero.

"A win-win for everyone."

"Yes, a win-win."

"When will you get it done?" Mensen asked.

"With my other duties, I'll need a couple of weeks to write a proposal. No guarantees, but it should get the ball rolling. The agency is slow, the regional office especially so. It's not like running a business." Rager did his best to sound sincere, but felt uncomfortable playing the role of a traitor. The Dutchman bought the act. Nonetheless, he felt cautious. Here was a very different man – not the self-righteous official on the mound telling him to "fuck off," but a man willing to take a bribe.

"Let's have a toast to the new partnership," Teddy said. He pulled a bottle of Cognac from one of the parka pockets. He held it up to the light so the amber liquid glowed. "Good stuff!" he said.

Rager retrieved two glasses from the closet. The Dutchman poured a good measure in each glass. Rager sipped his drink slowly. Mensen drank quickly, then poured himself another.

"You queer?" he asked.

"No. Why do you ask?"

"Makes no matter...but living alone, no woman, that's not normal. I only want to know what you like. I can get you anything – anything." He poured himself another drink. He looked around the room as though he were itemizing everything: side table, bureau, bookcase, and closet. His eyes were an intense cyan blue, piercing into every nook and cranny as though he were looking for evidence – if not a copy of the Torah, then some pornographic homosexual magazines. "If you want boys, I can get you boys," he said. "If you want a woman, I can get you a woman. You like to fuck a nice young girl, something soft and small, something cute, I can arrange that too. I arrange it for Freddy when he goes to Toronto, lots of girls to choose from in the city – Filipinos, Thai, Blacks, Indians, even Mexicans. Just let me know if you want the same thing. I can do it – I can do anything. I have good connections in Toronto." He talked as if he were selling apples, oranges, and melons.

"I'll let you know."

"What do you think about your new boss?"

"Not much."

"I agree. Gordon's a fool. I have one question: can we trust him?"

"No, we can't; but he's not important, not in the grand scheme of things. It's the regional office that decides if you get approval to buy the camps. It will be up to the regional superintendent of economic development, my superior, a man named Stephen Majors. He makes the final decision on whether the agency should sell the camps and, more importantly, whether the agency should provide a loan and contribution to renovate and modernize the camps and launch a promotion and marketing campaign. There is also the Indian Small Business Loan Advisory Board, which is ostensibly independent from government but in reality rubber-stamps whatever region recommends.

"I think that with the camps, Stephen will come around, especially if we provide a convincing proposal. We have to be careful, though. We can't make it look overly convincing. What we need is for Stephen to take it on for himself. They're not happy with me right now. I'm a pariah in the agency – it can't be my idea. Do you understand – it has to be *his* idea?"

"Yes," Teddy replied, though he was uncertain of why Rager was talking about man-eating fish in the Amazon jungle. He poured himself another drink and drank slower, the sweat still pouring down his red, bloated, porcine face. "You know, those accusations you made, not very smart. Nothing good came from that inspector's visit. The government don't care about Indians. Do you ever see those higher-ups from Toronto here in Grayson or the Indian villages? No, never. They stick to where they belong: in the cities. Of course, they only think of themselves. It's natural, a law of nature; look after yourself, that's what people do.

"Now, take you, John; you need to take better care of yourself. Why, you think you're going to get anything out of those big city people? No, you won't. They don't even like you, and if they could, they'd fire you on the spot. You know that, don't you?" Rager nodded in agreement. "Good – I don't make up stories. So, let's talk more about what I can do for you.

"I know you want to hear about money, but we have to be careful. I have a better idea than just money. You get money, but not now – later, after I get the camps and government funding. For now, I arrange a free trip for you to Nassau, one of those package tours with everything covered – hotel, meals, and air fare. I have a friend who runs a tour company; he will list you as a tour guide, so it says to anyone that checks that you work for the company. Plus, I give you some cash for spending money. Of course, you don't do any tour guiding – no work, just fun, and maybe you get some pussy on the side?

"I have another idea. We form a company with you as part-owner – say I give you twenty-five percent of the shares. We include some Indians as owners – say we give them ten percent of the shares. The company buys the Main Hotel in Grayson. You help the company get government funding to fix it up, add a stage and a dance floor, then we bring in strippers and you come on as the hotel manager. After a few years, we sell the business to an Indian band and pocket the profits."

"If I agree, it has to be done carefully. I want a contract stipulating what I get for securing the agency camps and government funding."

"Don't worry, no one will know. I have a good lawyer who knows how to do these sorts of contracts quietly." Mensen smiled, content with the offer and the apparent agreement. He noticed that the room was tidy and clean. There were no dirty cups or dishes, no basket full of laundry, only two books on the table with strange titles, *Our Winter of Discontent* and *Light In August*. He wondered if Rager belonged to a horticultural society.

"You like to read?" he asked.

"Yes, I do."

"I only read *Playboy* and *Hustler*."

With that, Teddy laughed and walked out of the room.

(2)

The proposal he crafted for the Dutchman outlined the benefits of turning over the ownership of the camps to the Mensen Air Charter Services Company for one dollar. He requested that the agency provide a one-million-dollar loan and a five-hundred-thousand-dollar contribution to renovate the camps and launch a promotion and marketing campaign. Essentially, he drafted the same proposal he had been working on for the Indian development corporation, with one notable exception: Mensen would be the sole owner of the camps and would earn all profits and management fees. After drafting the proposal, Mensen signed a covering letter and Rager forwarded the proposal to Stephen with a recommendation to approve the proposal, knowing that Stephen would take a number of weeks to reach a decision.

A short time later, Rager signed a contract with Mensen with a guarantee that he would receive an all-expense paid trip to Nassau for drafting the proposal, twenty-five percent ownership of the Main Hotel, and the position as hotel manager, conditional on the agency providing the funding. Should the contract ever be released to the media, it would bring into question the veracity of Tom Blackwell's report. What was missing was a report outlining how all the pieces fit together: a history of corrupt district officials accepting bribes; the beating of an Indian chief who spoke up; a contract promising lucrative benefits to a district official once the agency approved funding; and how the agency so easily rejected the possibility of Indian camp ownership over the ownership of a corrupt white operator.

The Nassau trip in mid-March was surreal. It began with a flight on a crowded charter flight that left Toronto after midnight and arrived in Nassau in the early predawn hours. Rager found it a strange experience, leaving a snow-covered airport at midnight with a plane full of animated revelers and arriving on a Caribbean Island three hours later in the predawn hours, with a soft ocean breeze. It was no less strange on Paradise Island. He was booked into a single room overlooking a pool in a new luxury hotel, a free bottle of rum and a basket of fruit on the coffee table. On the table was an invitation to a cocktail party in the afternoon and a list of discounted tours should he desire to go scuba diving, ride a glass-bottom boat to Rose Island, view a coral reef, or charter a sportfishing boat. There was also an invitation to the hotel casino to try his luck on the tables and slot machines.

After sleeping a couple of hours, he went down to have breakfast. He walked on the beach, swam in the pool, and tried his luck in the casino, but after losing at blackjack and the slot machines, he decided it would be best if he stuck to other activities. Throughout his stay he drank modestly. He spoke a few times with hotel guests sitting by the pool.

"Where are you from?" a woman asked.

"Canada," he answered.

"Isn't the weather wonderful?"

"Yes, it's wonderful," he replied.

"And the rum is so cheap."

"Yes, it's cheap."

"Have you taken a glass-bottom boat ride?"

"I went to Rose Island – very nice," he said.

"I did, too."

It was a common theme, people asking a few questions and then talking about the weather, inexpensive rum, and available tours. What was highly unusual were the knocks on his door in the middle of the night from different prostitutes offering their services. On the first night, his visitor was a young Filipino woman. "Hello, John, I'm Honey," she said before he chased her away. On the second night, it was a transsexual woman: "Hello, sweetie, are you looking for company?" she said before he chased her away. On the third night, it was a muscular man in tight shorts and a tee shirt. "The agency sent me," the man said in a deep, masculine voice before Rager chased him away. Finally, fed up with the unwanted attention, he phoned Teddy and told him to stop sending him prostitutes. The Dutchman replied, "I'm just sending you an assortment. You pick, you choose, everything is taken care of, no expense."

"No thanks, I'm not interested. Maybe another time. I like the swimming and gambling. Besides, I have my eye on a real beauty, a blond woman, *very* attractive. She sits by the pool every day; I think I have a good shot at getting her into the sack."

"Good. Enjoy yourself."

After the brief exchange, there were no more knocks on the door.

The week passed quickly. Rager's return flight was more subdued: a plane filled with worn-out, sunburned tourists returning to the frozen Canadian winter.

(3)

On his way back to Grayson, Rager arranged to spend two days in Toronto, stopping in to see Marie.

On the first day, he walked over to the women's shelter, where she was comforting a frightened, badly-beaten woman as her children cried. Later, Marie helped another woman find an apartment. Then she went off to the mayor's office to request more funding support. She commented, "I either counsel women, deal with the police, or write funding proposals. I would say that half my time is spent writing proposals. I don't think society really understands the important work that we do, without which you would have women and children living on the street. So much is hidden in society, so much is buried."

Rager told her about the trip to Nassau and the ridiculous late-night visits by prostitutes.

"One night it was a Filipino, the second night a transsexual, and the third night a muscular man."

"Was he attractive?" Marie asked mischievously.

"No, he was ugly. I phoned Mensen and told him to stop sending me prostitutes. I said that I had my eye on a blond woman."

"Was she attractive?"

"Jealous?"

"No. You are a free man."

"Am I?"

"Not if you don't want to be."

"I don't want to be free. I should have told Mensen that I have my eye on a former nun who knows how to tease."

She blew him a kiss.

He told her about his plan, and that he was keeping all trip receipts to show he never received payment as a tour guide, nor did he do any guiding – for one thing, it was his first trip to Nassau.

"What could I tell a tour group – perhaps that every night a prostitute will knock on your door? I'm also keeping a copy of the contract I signed with Mensen. The evidence should be enough to re-open an investigation into Mensen. I also intend to get Freddy and Olaf involved in the hotel scheme by telling them that if they invested, it would be an opportunity to earn big money, especially since Mensen intends to bring in strippers and hire me as a manager. Once it all comes out, I don't think the agency will be able to sweep it under the rug."

"Watch out for Mensen – or should I say, Mr. Rotmensen. A man like that might appear crude and stupid, but he is capable of doing almost anything. As I told you, he raped a fourteen-year-old Indian girl who now works on the streets in Winnipeg. He was also a member of the Waffen-SS. How many people do you think he shipped to the concentration camps? I don't think murder is beyond his capability."

"I will, believe me, but I don't scare easily."

Marie's apartment bedroom was magical. She had purchased a bureau that was covered with zebra and giraffe images and a bed with a white canopy; when a candle was lit and the incense burned, it seemed to Rager that he was in a tent on the African Serengeti. Who was this strange French-Canadian blond woman?

"Why are you here in the middle of the night, staring at the wall?" she asked.

He answered, "Because I'm deeply in love with you."

"Are you sure?"

"Yes."

They talked about the future. "I'm going to write this all up and connect the dots; not just between Mensen, the bribes, and Elijah's beating, but about the whole system that keeps the Indians of northwestern Ontario at the bottom of the economy. Everything needs to come out; every last piece of dirt and rot. I hope to pack my bags and get out of Grayson by June, if not earlier. I would like to move to Toronto and get a job. Maybe we could live together. I like your taste in furniture."

"My room is always open," Marie said.

When he said goodbye, he had a strange feeling, as though he might never see her again.

"No matter what happens, promise you won't forget me?" he asked.

"I won't forget you, John. I hope to see you again, and again, and again."

(4)

When Rager returned to the office in Grayson, he spoke with Freddy, telling him that he had made a stupid mistake accusing him and Olaf of beating up Elijah. "I'm very sorry and feel stupid for what I did. Everyone knows that Elijah is a drunk and a trouble-maker. Why I listened to what he said, I have no idea. I hope you can accept my apology."

"It's okay, because nothing came of it," Freddy replied.

Rager went on to say that he was tired of working for an agency that offered no prospect of advancement. "I don't think they want me to be anything but a commerce officer, so I've decided to partner with Mensen to buy the Main Hotel and serve as manager. We plan on renovating the hotel, adding a stage and dance floor, and bringing in strippers. Mensen wants a few token Indians as share-holders so we can access government funding. You and Olaf might want to invest. Think about it, I know there's going to be a lot of profit."

Freddy phoned Mensen, who was agreeable to Freddy and Olaf investing in the project. Within a week Rager was meeting with his two colleagues in the Legion as though there had never been any trouble between them. It amazed Rager how easily two fools could be won over once there was money to be made.

In early April, Stephen phoned to say that he supported the Dutchman's proposal. "It just makes sense," he said. "We provide the Mensen Air Charter Services Company with a loan and contribution, and the company renovates the camps to create employment and income for the villages. We should never have been in the sportfishing business. After all, what does the government know about running a tourism business? Not much."

There was never any mention of offering a similar opportunity to an Indian development corporation. As far as Stephen was concerned, the concept had never come up.

Chapter 2
JULIA

(1)

As soon as he arrived back in the district office, Rager began to draft his tell-all report. Late at night, alone in the office, he outlined the history of bribes in the district: how "good service" meant nothing more than what an official defined it to be; the beating of an Indian chief who complained about the bribes for a fuel contract; and the inspector's report that found no evidence. (Why were the chiefs at the district meeting not interviewed? What did they know about the system of bribes? Why was Marie Brunelle not interviewed since she too had heard about the system of bribes?)

In the report, Rager went on to describe the contract he signed with Mensen to write a proposal in exchange for an all-expense trip to Nassau, where he was listed as a 'tour guide' but did no guiding. Finally, he outlined the scheme to purchase the Main Hotel with token Indians as shareholders to secure agency funding. He documented the dates of meetings and travel, included ticket and hotel receipts showing he paid nothing, and a copy of the signed contract.

Rager typed the report on a portable typewriter and hid the document in one of the side drawers, thinking that no one ever looked into his desk. But he was wrong. One person did take notice of his typing alone at night – an unusual activity, since all the letters and reports were typed by clerk-secretaries.

The district office manager was a cold and bitter woman who stared out at the world from a closed-in office through a glazed window into the faces of much younger, more attractive clerk-secretaries. Mrs. Winters, or Julia, could hardly speak to anyone without her thin, reed-like voice sounding threatening. "You and I need to talk privately," she would say and disappear into her office to pull out an expense claim where the official was attempting to claim expenses that were not allowed under Treasury Board Guidelines.

Julia seemed to have always been the office manager; someone from long before, when there had only been her and Mr. Reed. She knew everything about the office and kept everything to herself – unless, of course, there was a reason to speak up.

Julia found Rager's secret report hidden in the side drawer where all the previous commerce officers had kept confidential documents. She had always looked through desks when officers were travelling. She read and copied Rager's report. It was one she would share.

(2)

When Julia drove out on a Saturday afternoon to the Mensen Air Services Company float base, there were already deep ruts on the gravel road, so she drove slowly and carefully. When she reached the office, the lake was still frozen, with Mensen sitting alone in the office drinking and brooding. All he could think about was what she had said on the phone.

"Teddy, he's written a report on everything: the free trip you paid for, the hotel, everything. He even has receipts and a copy of the contract you both signed. It looks very bad for you!" She sounded mean and spiteful, as though she enjoyed telling him.

"Get me a copy of the report and bring it to me, pronto," he instructed. After he hung up, he felt panicked and started to drink.

When she arrived, Julia parked the car and approached the office. She knocked on the door. "Come in," he said coldly.

The Dutchman was stretched out on a sofa with a beer in hand. He seemed larger, more bloated, and he stank of alcohol; even if he whispered, the stench filled the room. He pointed to a wooden chair – "Sit!" he commanded. She handed him the report and sat down. These two people knew they must do their best to get along before parting, hoping not to see each other unless out of necessity.

Mensen took his time to read the report. Occasionally he grunted and swore – "Bastard! Weasel! Cunt!" – and drank as much as he spilled. Julia, a thief more interested in money than anything else, watched without saying a word. She had long been Mensen's informant. He returned the favour by occasionally dropping off an envelope with two or three hundred-dollar bills in her mailbox. This was not much money for the Dutchman, but for a woman living alone on a small government salary and facing the prospect of living off a much smaller pension, it was a great deal of money. She called his payments her "lottery money." In addition to giving her more security, it served as a symbol of her power to betray – she often imagined herself as a Mata Hari, sneaking around to discover secrets. She was good at spying. It suited her as much as her cheap polyester suit and tasteless brown shoes and the hate she felt for those who were more attractive.

When Mensen finished, he said, "I'll have to kill him."

"You can't be serious, Teddy."

"I am serious. Fucking weasel! Fucking coward!"

He stared at her as though she had spoken out of turn. "How come I only hear of this now?"

"I didn't know, Teddy. I promise you I didn't know. Who would know? He always works alone. It was really lucky that I overheard him typing and wondered what he was doing. I found the report only by snooping and checking through his desk. I was lucky – very lucky. He could have kept it somewhere else."

"Everyone cheats and lies in that office – maybe you, too?" He looked at Julia as though he would have to beat her.

"Not me, Teddy. No. No way. "

"Everyone else does, why not you?"

"No. I would never betray you. Never!"

Mensen let it rest. He could strangle or beat Rager to death; either way it would give him pleasure to see the man suffer and die. He stood and gave Julia two hundred dollars. "Here. Go, and don't say a word to anyone, you understand?"

"I won't tell anyone."

"Forget what I said. I won't hurt Mister Rager. I only tease. You know that – tease." He gave her a weak smile.

"Yes, I know you don't mean what you say." She left without saying another word. It was a great relief to be out of the office. She felt as though she had just avoided a beating. She drove back to Grayson. She kept the money she earned from Mensen in a jar to play in the government lottery.

Besides Rager's report, the Dutchman had more than enough troubles to keep his mind occupied. The chart paper on the wall that recorded the seasonal bookings had too many blanks; it would make back-to-back flights challenging. An increase in operating expenses was squeezing profits, and the bank might reduce his operating loan. His proposal to purchase the sixteen agency tourist camps would only succeed if the agency provided one and a half million dollars in funding, but it would take time to generate increased revenues. Still, he believed it would all work out, as long as the ownership transfer went smoothly and the agency provided the funding.

Rager's report placed all of that in jeopardy. Once released, the report would lead to another investigation, another inspector's visit, and a possible audit. With enough probing the auditors would find that he had provided free trips and bribes to a long list of government officials, just as Rager outlined in his report. It could lead to criminal charges. There were also the legal costs of hiring a lawyer and a long, drawn-out court case. It would only be a matter of time before Mensen was bankrupt, if not in jail – the government did not take kindly to those who conspired to steal from its coffers, especially a former member of the Waffen-SS.

Mensen had a way of thinking that went back a long way. Even before the war, as a child growing up, he was different – a greedy boy, a bully who always had to have his way. Perhaps that is why, alone in the office, knowing that everything might come crashing down, he tore out the phone, smashed the furniture, and pounded his fist through the paneling until he finally passed out. It all seemed a great relief when he was no longer conscious, as though the act of thinking was a great misery, a great boil to be lanced.

Chapter 3
FLYING NORTH

(1)

Rager did not have allies – certainly not in the agency. He was a man who worked alone in the back of a district office. It was true that he got along well with the Indians – some, like Gordon, saw him as an "Indian-lover" – and that he had found Marie, but ultimately he was alone. He thought things would all work out; he would finish his secret report, add a few final comments, a few *bon mots*, and then send it off to the *Chronicle-Journal* in Thunder Bay, the *Globe and Mail* in Toronto, and the RCMP.

But things never did work out – not even close.

On a late Friday afternoon in mid-May, Mensen phoned and invited Rager to fly north to inspect one of the agency camps. "I'm flying to Arrow Lake camp tomorrow to deliver fuel and outboard motors and to inspect the cabins. Why not come along? We can talk about the contribution and loan, the Main Hotel, and when you can start. At the same time, we can do some fishing and have a couple of beers, just the two of us, no one else. I guarantee that you'll have a good time."

The Dutchman seemed friendly, but the invitation was a pretext. Mensen had already decided what he would do, and it would not be pretty. He would wait until they were alone to confront Rager and explain to him carefully that the only path forward – the safest, the most prudent, and the most profitable – was to bury the report. "I can hurt you worse than you know, worse than you can imagine! If you only knew what I have done in the past, you would not think twice what you're planning." That was what he would say and, if need be, he would squeeze the man's neck again. Mensen wanted to scare him, to make Rager understand that death was imminent if he crossed the Dutchman.

If anything, Mensen understood how to isolate and bully a weaker man, make him cry, make him beg for his life, even kill him. He would wait and see what was the most effective course of action. Terror was a wonderful thing – a bully's magic wand – and he loved to use the wand. Killing – throwing a man out of a plane and claiming he jumped – was also easily done. "He was very depressed," he would tell the police. "He talked crazy, *loco*, it was all about losing his job and people turning against him. I tried to tell him it would pass, but I never thought he would jump. He was alone in the back of the plane. When I looked back, I only saw the open door. I was the pilot. I was alone. How could I know he would jump? But he did. It was terrible, but what could I do, and who would think a man would do such a thing – no one!"

Rager drove up on the gravel road that was full of potholes, deep ruts, and mounds of gravel waiting for the arrival of a grader. When he arrived at the float base, the pilots and dock boys were busy loading planes, with Mensen standing on the mound yelling and directing traffic. "What took you so long? I got things to do," he said, no longer as friendly as when he phoned.

"The road was in terrible shape."

"Always is this time of year – you should know that by now." He looked annoyed but managed a smile. "Okay, let's go. Time's a-wasting."

He pointed to the single-engine Otter. It was the same plane that Rager had flown in on his flight to Windsor House the previous fall. The plane's floats rested deep in the water, just above the water line. "We're taking forty-five-gallon drums of gasoline and outboard motors, so it's a full load. Arrow Lake is three hundred and fifty kilometers north and one hundred and fifty kilometers south of Hudson Bay. Depending on head winds, the flight should take one and a half hours. We fly at twelve thousand feet. The weather is good. No stops; it's a straight line there and back. Once we get to the lake, we unload the fuel and engines, inspect the cabins, see what has to be done, then we can spend a couple of hours fishing, have a couple of beers, and talk. We should be back in five or six hours. If the weather changes, we have enough fuel to reach the float base with an extra hour, give or take."

Rager boarded the plane and sat in the co-pilot's seat. The Dutchman untied and pushed the plane free from the dock, boarded, and took the pilot's seat. At the last moment, he yelled at a pilot to return by a specified time. "Get the work done and get back! No delay, you understand?" He seemed to enjoy bullying, even as he was leaving. The pilot nodded. Mensen whispered under his breath, "Asshole!" It was the way he felt about everyone.

Mensen ignited the engine, which made the familiar sputtering and coughing sounds followed by a roar. He handed Rager a set of earmuffs. Once they were on, neither man could hear the other. The Dutchman steered the plane out onto the lake and, finally, up into the air.

When they reached twelve thousand feet, he set the auto pilot, reached back to a case of beer, took out a bottle, and began to drink. He motioned to his one passenger to help himself, but Rager declined, leaving the Dutchman to drink alone. Throughout the rest of the trip, Mensen continued to drink while reading a newspaper and throwing the pages into the cargo hold. At one point, he looked outside and noticed a flock of geese, cocked his fingers as though shooting, and turned and aimed at Rager, leaving no doubt of his intention. It was just the beginning of what was to come.

Rager began to think, "Does he know of my report – but how? What if he becomes drunk, incapacitated, what will I do?" He began to count the number of beers the Dutchman consumed – "Three so far. I wonder how many more he had before we left?" By the time they reached the lake, the Dutchman had consumed two more beers and by then appeared cheery, even whistling – a drunk with a bloated face, flying and landing a plane without a care in the world, or so it seemed. It was hard to know what Mensen was thinking, if anything. Rager only became more deeply worried as he read the signs.

They began their descent. They flew over the rapids that separated the lake from the river, over the mound where the camp was situated – cook house, guide cabin, and two guest cabins – and descended over the shore where there was a shed, a dock, a stack of empty fuel drums, and six overturned aluminum boats. There were no other tourist camps on the lake. There was only the wilderness, a vast world of green and blue.

After they landed, they tied the plane and unloaded the gasoline drums and outboard motors. Mensen moved awkwardly. He almost stumbled and fell into the rapids, but somehow managed to straighten himself up and regain a degree of sobriety. He pointed to the cabins. "Let's see how bad they are." He walked up to the cabins and Rager followed.

The buildings were in terrible shape: there were leaky roofs and broken doors; the cook house had a broken table, stained walls, rusted fridge, an oil burner leaking oil; and the guest and guide cabins had stained mattresses, cracked windows, and broken furniture. Mensen grew angry. "I'll have to send a crew in to fix the fucking place up," he said. "It's going to cost me plenty! Anyway, we need to do it. I can't wait, I have bookings. Better have that agency funding ready, otherwise I'm calling everything off, you understand?" He was clearly upset with the condition of the camp and the delay in receiving the agency funding.

"As soon as I get back to the office," Rager replied, "I'll follow up with Stephen and find out what's holding up the loan and contribution funding."

"Good. I don't want to hear any more about delays, you understand me?"

Rager nodded that he understood. He added, "Stephen's already approved the proposal, so it's only the Small Business Advisory Board that we're waiting for. They have to give their final approval, but don't worry, it's only a short delay. I expect to receive the documents any day in the mail. I'll get them to you as soon as I can and you can sign them. The money should flow soon after."

But Mensen was not pleased. "I can't wait – I need the money. I need it, like, yesterday. The season is opening up, and I have to send in a repair crew. There are the other camps, too. If they're in the same shape as this one, it's going to take money and time to ready them. What do you expect me to do, wait and do nothing? Besides, I don't even know if I own the camps. There are too many loose ends in this whole fucking thing." He glared at Rager as though he were ready to strike him." Why have I not gotten anything except your reassurance that it's all happening? How do I know it's not bullshit?"

"Well, you *are* getting the camps and you *are* getting the funding. You just have to be patient. What about the bank? What if I speak to your bank manager, let him know what's happening? Maybe he'll approve a bridge loan."

"I'm already over-extended."

"Well, I'm certain I can arrange something." Rager repeated his offer. "When I'm back in the office, I'll phone and speak with Stephen. I'll explain that you can't wait. I'll push him to speed things up."

"You better, you understand?"

"I do understand. I hope that you also understand my position. I'm trying my best, Teddy, you know that."

"Oh, I bet you are."

There was no signed contribution agreement, and no loan agreement. Although Stephen had said he supported the proposal, the documents needed to be signed and the security taken on the loan before funds were released; none of these documents had yet been sent. Further, the Indian Small Business Loan Fund Advisory Board would have to approve the loan. Although this seemed a formality, much like everything else in the agency, good or bad, everything took time, even if failure could be prevented with speed, there was always a committee or a senior official who needed to approve a decision. There was always the paperwork and the legal requirements. Everyone knew this, Rager perhaps more than others, and so did Mensen.

The Dutchmen whistled. He pointed to a coffee pot lying on the floor. "Let's have some coffee and clear our heads."

"Sure," Rager replied, relieved that the angry tone of questioning had stopped.

Mensen staggered down to the lake, returned with a pot full of water, and placed it on the gas stove. Rager turned away and looked out a broken window. "Felt like a long trip?" Mensen commented.

"Yes, a very long trip. I'm glad we're finally on the ground."

"You like this sort of work?" Mensen asked.

"Not crazy about the government side of the work. Everything takes so long, but there's not much anyone can do. The government has all these checks and balances; they just don't trust anyone, and they certainly don't delegate decision-making. I can't take a trip or buy a pencil without getting prior approval. I'll be glad when I'm out of the government."

The Dutchman began to whistle again. There was an eerie quality to his demeanor. "What you do late at night, John, all alone in your office?"

Rager felt the man's hand reaching around his neck.

"What do you mean?"

"What do I mean? You like to write stories – yes, I think so. Funny make-believe stories? Oh, I think you do."

"What are you trying to tell me?"

"You know Julia?"

"Yes, of course, our office manager."

"Well, Julia works for me, and she showed me your *secret* report – all about our little arrangement, the contract, and the trip to Nassau. You even have receipts from the trip and a copy of the contract. Why do you write this stuff, John? Why?" He pulled Rager around to peer into his eyes, as though he were a goat tied to a stake, waiting for slaughter.

At that point, Rager knew it was no longer possible to continue the lie. He chose his words carefully. "If you've read my report, then you know what I think. The camps belong to the Indian bands. You, on the other hand, are nothing but a cheat, a liar, a bully, and from what I've been told, a man with a terrible past. Tell me, Teddy, how did it feel loading the Jews onto the trains going to the concentration camps – all those men, women, and children wondering where they were going? Did you shoot people, did you laugh, did it give you pleasure? What about the

Indian girl you raped? Let's talk about her, or did that, too, get buried like everything else? Did you really think you could buy me off? Do you think a trip to Nassau or a twenty-five percent stake in a dump – with strippers, no less – would change my way of thinking?" He laughed. "Well, let me tell you, it doesn't! You should go to jail, you son-of-a bitch!"

"So you say."

"So I say."

The Dutchman slapped Rager across the face, leaving a deep, burning mark. The smaller man stood without saying a word.

"Oh, you want more?" He slapped him again.

"Fuck you," Rager said.

The water in the coffee pot began to whistle; it seemed to be a signal for a compromise. The Dutchman went over and turned the gas off on the stove. It was suddenly dead quiet. Rager could hear a bird chirping outside. "Why do you want to do this, John?" Mensen asked. "You know I can't let this happen. You know I could hurt you."

"Go ahead, hurt me. If you think I'm scared, well, I'm not. I never have been scared of you. I never will be!"

The Dutchman punched Rager in the face as hard as he could, twisted him around, and placed him in a choke hold, squeezing until he passed out. Then he dragged Rager outside and tied him to a tree.

At that point, he turned his attention to loading the plane with empty fuel drums. As he worked, he mumbled to himself, "I'm going to teach the fucking little weasel a good lesson, just like we taught the Jews.

You start something against me, I finish it. Oh, I'm going to have fun." He continued mumbling to himself until he was finished loading. He returned, untied Rager from the tree, and poured water onto the man's face until he regained consciousness.

It came slowly. "What are you doing?" Rager asked.

"Shut up! Shut the fuck up! Are you going to tear up the report and be a good boy?"

"No."

"No? That is the last word you will ever say to me!" The Dutchman smashed his fist into Rager's face and broke his jaw. Rager's head began to spin. The Dutchman hit him again. Then he watched him squirming and groaning. "I tell you not to talk, just listen. You're going to do what I tell you. You're going to tear up that report, you're going to have no report – nothing! Mister, you are going to be good. You going to work for me."

Rager tried to speak; only a whisper came out of his mouth.

"What did you say?"

He attempted to gurgle. "No."

"Well, it doesn't matter. This is over."

The Dutchman grabbed him, turned him over like a rag doll, and tied his hands together so it was impossible to resist. "Stand up!" he said. Without waiting, Mensen lifted him up and pushed him as though he were a prisoner. Rager was a man with a broken jaw, his eyes swelled so badly he could hardly see, and he could feel nothing but the bigger man's arms around his chest, lifting and pushing, at times leaning his knee into his legs as though he were taking him to a cell instead of a floatplane tied to a dock.

Once they boarded, Mensen pushed him into the cargo hold, forced him down onto the floor, and tied his hands to a rail. When Rager tried to speak, he was told, "Shut up!" Mensen went out, untied the plane, returned, took his place in the pilot's chair, and radioed another pilot. Rager could barely hear the men speaking. "I'm flying north to inspect another camp before heading back," Mensen said.

"Sounds good, Teddy. See you later, ten-four," the pilot replied.

Why would Mensen fly north? It made no sense. But Rager had stopped thinking about what the Dutchman would or wouldn't do. He was unpredictable and capable of anything, even murder. Rager suddenly understood that the Dutchman intended to throw him out of the plane.

In a few minutes, they were airborne with the plane rolling along in the sky. The wind whistling outside softly. After a few minutes, Mensen set the auto-pilot and walked back to the cargo hold. He opened the loading door, then untied Rager's hands.

"Stand up! We go for a walk," he commanded.

At the door, Rager could see the lake far below.

"Look, John, there's the new camp site. See?!"

Without thinking, Rager fell to the side and kicked. It was just enough for Mensen to lose his footing and fall out of the plane.

There was no scream, no sound, only the wind.

"What have I done?" Rager thought.

The plane continued to roll. He was suddenly alone. His hands were tied, but he was free to move. Somehow, he managed to untie his hands and close the cargo door. He moved to the front and took the pilot's seat.

Rager knew very little about flying a plane; time and time again, he had watched different pilots flying planes, but he knew very little about the procedures. He grabbed the radio mike and attempted to speak, but his voice was weak and all he could hear on the speaker was static. He looked at the altimeter: it recorded eight thousand feet. He looked at the compass: the needle pointed north. How could he turn the plane around? He had no idea. There was nothing to do but stay conscious and steer the plane – perhaps down onto a lake, but how? He looked through Mensen's briefcase for an operating manual, but there were only maps and receipts and flight records.

He walked to the cargo hold and sat on the floor. All he could feel was the terrible pain in his jaw and the rolling of the plane. All he could think was that he was facing death.

He returned to the cockpit and waited. He thought he might faint, but the fear of death – the certainty of death – kept him focused. He was a man unable to pilot a plane and waiting to die.

Will it be soon?

Yes.

Will I feel pain?

No.

Will I remember who I was and what I did?

No.

Where will I crash?

Below, far below.

He thought about Sam. The boy would be nine. What would he be doing now that it was spring? Would he grow up to be an angry, lonely man unable to find happiness, or would he triumph? Rager hoped and prayed for the latter. Helen had married the wrong man, and he wished her well with her new partner.

He thought about his mother. "Where are you, Mother? Are you drinking alone this Saturday afternoon? Is the man down the hall bothering you?"

He thought about swimming on the lake and listening to the loons; the quiet afternoons in the sun, when nothing mattered. He thought about Bristol and the shantytown and wondered how many of the Indians would still be living there, and where their children might be. He thought about everything that mattered and let the rest slip away – Mr. Reed, Gordon, Freddy, Olaf, Stephen, and David – none of them mattered, not anymore. Did he see Mr. Reed, driving back with his wife from Florida? Did he see Gordon, still dreaming of Ottawa? Did he see Freddy and Olaf, drinking and laughing in the Legion bar? Did he see Stephen and Catherine, riding their bicycles along a quiet city street? Did he see their kind scattered in government offices across the country? Did he see Mensen lying dead far below, his head smashed into rocks?

He thought of Marie. "I wish I had known you before, when I was young and before you became a nun. Why did I never meet you? Why did my life have to end this way?"

"Love me…Love me," he said. *"Never forget me."*

"I never will."

Rager breathed quietly.

He accepted the inevitable.

The plane continued to roll through the sky. At some point, the auto-pilot failed and he watched as the plane began to descend into the wilderness, the Blue Forest. This was as it should be. He lay back in the pilot's seat, not moving, only hearing the sound of the wind. He saw nothing and felt nothing; only the great falling and the great freedom. John Rager's last words were, "It is finished."

(2)

The clouds, the stars, the northern lights, the water that laps, the million trees that brush and bend, the breathing that is deep within – life surrounds and engulfs with spirit and spirit moves and caresses like a dream that watches a dreamer. There is only the wilderness…only the green and blue…only life…

Slowly, timelessly, the river feeds through the trees, bush, earth, primeval ooze. In the far, far distance, the river fades, fades, dark and silt-saturated, past mud-flats on a coast where a million geese sleep, and quickly, quickly loses itself in the ocean that is cold, deep, and frightening. A whale surfaces. A seagull circles the leviathan.

The river moves through the wilderness. It comes from the air, the clouds, and the earth. It moves through lakes, through bogs, through forest, through marshy ground, and through the endless lakes and creeks.

It passes the villages that are quiet, poor, and forgotten.

It passes the outpost camps that are many and ancient – few maps record their presence.

In different forms, the river passes all these places.

It changes form in the fall and winter.

It feeds the people.

It is the people.

The plane and the two men's bodies were never found – neither Mensen's nor Rager's – in the Hudson Bay lowlands. They were thought to have died together somewhere in the great boreal wilderness – the Blue Forest.

(3)

The new commerce officer for the Indian Affairs Thunder Bay super district drove to Grayson looking for the former Nakina district office. He had been in his position for four months. He thought it was time to see for himself how the office appeared, now that he worked in a super district where the doors were always locked and protected. When he arrived in Grayson, he discovered a small federal building housing a post office, a tall Catholic church at the back, and a closed and shuttered CN train station across the street. He spoke with a man walking out of the post office. "I understand that Indian Affairs once had an office on the second floor. Do you know what the space is used for now?"

"It's a gym," the man replied. "After they left, a businessman purchased the building and turned the office into a small gym. Mind you, there are not many members. But what else could he do with the building? He kept the first floor and rented the space to the post office. I suppose he has a long-term lease. Why else would he have bought the building? A government long-term lease is like gold. The government should have bought the building, but you know how it is with the government; they spend money any way they want, whether it makes sense or not. The owner probably makes a good profit on the government lease. The gym is icing on the cake. The man who owns the building lives out of town. We never see him."

In the years that followed, life in the district Indian villages became far worse than anyone could ever have imagined. Unemployment and welfare climbed higher than anywhere else in the province. Housing was dismal – the district chiefs and councils continued to complain about overcrowded houses, mold that made people sick, and inadequate space for children to study. In the five fly-in villages, hundreds of people were addicted to Oxycontin and most of the villages were under a water advisory, with bottled water flown in daily – a great irony in a district where water, the "spring of life," flowed every-where. But then, no one seemed to know why this was so, least of all the Indian Affairs officials who blamed the problem on the Indians themselves, claiming they were incompetent at managing water treatment plants, even though an outside expert considered the water treat-ment plants the worst he had ever seen in any developed country. But then, no one seemed to question why Indian Affairs, which had changed its name and grown to a much larger bureaucracy, took forever to rectify the problem. In one village alone, bottled water had to be flown into the village for twenty-seven years and the problem was still not corrected.

Everyone seemed to forget the residential schools until the Truth and Reconciliation Commission came out with its findings and recommendations. Even then, the government took time to implement those recommendations. It was only when the burial sites of hundreds of children popped up out west in Kelowna – evidence of the genocide of a people – that the government started to take things more seriously. They had been doing this for a long time. It was in their blood, the practice of promising and then forgetting, and they seemed to continue the practice.

How high could a mediocre man like Stephen Majors climb in the government? In less than two years, he replaced David Stewart – who returned to academia to teach and write books – before taking a senior policy position with Treasury Board in Ottawa. Then Stephen Majors was appointed Assistant Deputy Minister of Supply and Services, and then Deputy Minister of Indian Affairs and Northern Development, before reaching the position of Clerk to the Privy Council, the highest-level position in the federal bureaucracy. When the incoming prime minister was given three people to choose for the position, two men and one woman, he initially chose the woman but was persuaded it was the wrong choice – "She is rather strong-minded, sir." And then there was Stephen: quiet, travelled, educated, had worked with Indigenous people, and knew how to "get along" and "make things work," so he was given the position and, after retirement, the Order of Canada.

And so, the country rested, even after all the dead Indigenous children were found in unmarked graves near residential schools.

What happened to the district chiefs? Some died of old age, others withered and died slowly, painfully, like branches on a tree. Others lived in the villages or moved away to cities like Thunder Bay until their hearts and spirits died, exhausted by the effort and knowledge that nothing would ever change – the plight of their people only got worse and worse.

In the end, it was always the *Shuniah-Ogama*, the Money Boss; the ones who gave or kept the gold, dollars, sticks, and stones who triumphed. They were never touched; they only grew in number and continued, happy to see their kind multiply.

As for the future? No one had an answer, only hundreds of recommendations like leaves falling on the ground – the ground of the Money Boss. Even Jesus, throwing the money lenders out of the temple, would weep and curse.

So it was that after nearly fifty years, the district Indians were a great deal far worse off than when a gentle, foolish man drove along a highway, wondering to himself what to expect as he entered Grayson for the first time.

What happened to John Rager's report? Julia never said anything. She burned the report. She knew it would raise too many unnecessary and difficult questions.

Chapter 4
A STRANGE NAME FOR ANYONE

The elderly woman often travelled to the lake near Grayson. She would rent a cabin at one of the lodges and stay for a couple of weeks. She did this at the end of summer, after Labour Day, when there were no mosquitoes, blackflies, or no-see-ums. She had been doing this for a number of years.

In the early morning, when the mist first appeared, before others were out on the lake, the woman climbed into a kayak and began paddling to a place where the reeds stood out. She paddled slowly to one of the bays where the lake was shallow and mud-bottomed, where the water flowed from across the highway, below the highway, below the earth, a deep mystery that continuously filled the lake.

She knew if she paddled far enough, she would come to the spot where the creek fills the lake, where the water is too shallow for boats, even canoes, but not a kayak, where the water is barely a few inches deep. She understood the lake as much as anyone can understand a living, breathing creature that changes before your eyes.

She was small, five feet and three inches in height, and her beautiful white hair had a shaggy cut, tucked back tight in a band. She could have been an *Obachan*, a grandmother, long accustomed to working in a rice field, but she was French-Canadian, staying at a small cottage on the lake and living alone.

The woman paddled slowly. She passed two loons with their chick; an eagle circling high above in the sky, hunting; all the time, paddling slowly through the mist, like a spirit finding its way through a cloud.

The woman was feeling her age. Her hands were arthritic, and a searing pain ran through her hands and fingers when bending the joints – yet she continued to paddle, not letting the pain stop her. Every morning when the sun was starting to rise, when life on the lake was beginning to move, she would kayak.

Her husband had died a number of years earlier. Aside from the summers when she came to the lake, she lived in Thunder Bay, near a beautiful park overlooking Lake Superior – a lake that was almost an inland sea. People came from all over the city to sit in their cars and watch the harbour below, with the ships arriving and leaving, and the Sleeping Giant, *Nanabijou*, in the distance, ready to rise at any moment.

As the woman drew near to the end of the bay, she stopped, rested her paddle, and lit a cigarette. She smoked slowly and thought, "John, you would have loved to be here. Yes, you would have loved to go kayaking in the morning, you in your own kayak and me beside you in mine, just the two of us paddling together. You would have loved to see the mist rising, you would have loved the mystery, the feeling of discovery, and finding your way."

In her mind, he was like a beautiful animal, a hidden animal like a lynx in the forest or an otter hidden deep in the water. A creature you only see now and then, a smart animal, a strong animal.

The man she was thinking about was not her dead husband, but a man she had known briefly before his tragic death, a man she always remembered. Later, she had married a good and decent man, had a child and led a long and peaceful life, eventually seeing her daughter move away, marry, and start her own family, and then watching her husband die slowly and painfully of cancer. But now she was alone and remembered an earlier time, before she was married, when her life lay before her. "Yes, John, you would have liked to be here. I think of you now, often. Nothing went well after you died. Everything got worse, much worse. But you probably knew that it would. I think you always knew more than you let on." And then she continued to paddle along the lake, with the mist rising and the sun beginning to push the mist far away.

Marie Brunelle died in Thunder Bay, Ontario, on April 12, 2020. On her death bed, she mumbled about a man she had known who had died in a plane crash. No one could make out the man's name – it sounded like "Rage." A strange name for anyone.

Lightning Source UK Ltd.
Milton Keynes UK
UKHW010636270123
416064UK00001B/234